For my dad, wh

Chapter One

If you looked at a souvenir photo taken at the start of our rafting trip down the Lehigh River, you'd say we were having a great time. You'd see the five of us—Mr. and Mrs. Browning, Suzi Browning, Jan Flower, and me, Abby Morrell—all smiling and gripping our paddles, ready to conquer the river.

But it all went wrong after we made one sharp turn into rushing rapids. There was no way to know at the start that I'd soon be in serious trouble, or that a boy named Kirk Phillips would come barreling into my life, or that from then on nothing would ever be the same. . . .

"Hang on tight, girls! Grab the ropes, or you'll be swept out of the raft—"

I could hear somebody shouting, but I couldn't be sure who it was. Mr. Browning? His wife? All I

1

knew was that I was moving my paddle in that frothing white-river water, but I was losing control. We all were.

The raft just ahead of us had slammed into a rock and was hung up on it. Foaming water splashed hard at the six people inside. Our raft locked with theirs, and the next thing I knew . . . icy water was pouring in all around us.

"Get out on the rock and hang on," Mr. Browning called out. Everything happened so fast that I can hardly remember the sequence. But I saw Suzi and Jan jump on the rock, and I watched in horror as Mr. and Mrs. Browning went tumbling into the rushing river.

"We'll be fine, Abby, don't worry about us" was the last thing I heard Mrs. Browning say as she floundered around, secure in her life jacket.

"We can swim," her husband said, trying not to swallow water.

That was when my raft suddenly tore away from the rock and started bumping down the river. I was completely alone.

This can't be happening, I thought. I forced myself to take a deep breath to calm myself. But no one could have been calm in that nightmare!

As I bounced down the river, I realized I had no hope of controlling a huge raft with water rushing into it.

You're not going to make it, kiddo, a little inner voice taunted me.

Shut up, I said back. *I'm not finished yet!*

And that was when Kirk Phillips climbed into my raft.

He didn't charge in like Superman or the U.S. Marines. No, he was panting hard, exhausted from fighting the river. And he was every bit as scared as I was.

He rolled in with a thump, splashing water all over.

"Where did you come from?" I screamed over the noise of the river. "I thought I'd never see another human being in this raft again."

"Hey this is a lot better than the situation I just left. The rock tore completely through our raft, and it's totally unsalvageable," Kirk screamed back. "I was swept off the rock." He was one of those cool juniors who had been having water fights back in the calm sections.

"What do we do?" he asked, his big brown eyes wide.

"I have no idea," I answered not too calmly.

In spite of my terror, I stared at him for a minute—tall and blond and strong-looking— and I felt a little better. Just a little.

At least he was *somebody.* I wasn't alone anymore.

Our raft rushed on deeper into the rapids,

bumping into boulders as though it were the ball in a pinball machine.

I yelled to him, "We have only one paddle, right?"

"Looks that way. Would you like me to paddle?"

I leaned across the half-submerged raft and gave him the paddle. We both winced as our boat crashed once again.

"Can you bail? Do you still have a bucket?" Kirk was still panting, fighting against the river's many currents. "It's impossible to maneuver with all this water."

I blinked. He was right, of course. Now that he was holding the paddle, I was free to bail. I grabbed the bucket, which had miraculously remained in the raft, and started scooping frantically.

I began to hope that we weren't doomed after all.

"What's happening to the others?" I asked as we whizzed along the river, flanked on both sides by steep cliffs as gray as headstones. I was worried about the Brownings and Jan and Suzi, my two best friends.

"Can't see anything back there anymore," Kirk answered. "But the guide boat will pick them up. That's why they have that last raft full of professionals."

I sighed and kept on scooping, dumping out water.

"I think we're gaining, Abby." Kirk sounded triumphant. "We haven't taken in any more water, and we seem to be getting the knack of running this thing with only one paddle."

I was surprised; I never imagined Kirk Phillips would know my name. How would a popular junior boy know me, a quiet, unremarkable sophomore?

I scooped some more, feeling a slight redness creep up around my cheeks. "You might be right," I answered brightly.

"But this ride ain't over yet," he said, trying to grin and sound like a hillbilly, which he definitely wasn't.

We bounced along, still scared out of our minds, but tried to act calm—as though this were something we did every day. The truth was, of course, this was the first river raft trip for either of us.

And my last, I was thinking. We were gaining on another raft that looked as if it was having no trouble. "Ask them for a paddle," I shouted to Kirk. He tried, but no one could hear him.

"Let's both yell," he suggested. We raised our voices as loud as we could. "Please—can you spare a paddle? We'll sink if we don't get control here."

Finally one woman threw us her paddle, and we thanked her profusely.

"Here you go, lady," Kirk said, throwing the paddle toward me. "Now maybe we'll have a chance."

"I'll do my best," I declared, wishing I were stronger because the current was so wild.

"I know you will." Kirk looked amused. "You're doing fine, Abby."

I began blushing stupidly. How *did* he know my name, anyway?

We finally hit a stretch of calm water, where the sun sparkled on the bright green, nonthreatening swirls and ripples. Both of us breathed sighs of relief. "Well, what happens now? Are we going to make it to the finish?" I asked as I crawled forward to paddle opposite him.

"Of course we are." Kirk turned and gave me a dazzling smile. "Did we ever doubt it?"

And that was our cue to laugh, crazily and hysterically. I knew that I should still be scared, because it wasn't over yet, but I was feeling almost relaxed. I watched the way the shadows and sunlight were flickering on Kirk Phillips's thick, wavy hair, making flecks of gold dance in the wet strands.

It also had something to do with the way his brown eyes were fixed intently on me, much more than they should have been when he had a raft to keep afloat.

He sat forward on his side of the bobbing craft. "You know, Abby, you look awfully cute right now."

"Oh, sure. My hair and clothes are soaked! I must be real big competition for Brooke Shields," I blathered. I had to make a wisecrack, or I probably would have fallen overboard. That's how shocked I was. Kirk Phillips giving *me* a compliment? I stared down at my soggy sneakers and swallowed hard, because I didn't want to look at him.

He didn't mean a word of it; I knew that. I was no dummy. I looked like a drowned rat, nowhere near cute at that point.

"Hey, Abby, I—" But he should have been paying more attention to his rafting. We swept so close to the river's edge that Kirk's head was brushed by some overhanging branches.

"Whoa!" he howled. "Could have had my head chopped off that time!"

But quickly enough he recovered and smiled, staring over at me again. "We saved each other's lives, Abby." There was a solemn expression in his dark eyes.

I forced myself to chuckle lightly. "That's right, we did. I guess that makes us blood brothers."

His eyebrows lifted. "Brothers? I wouldn't say that. You don't look like any of my brothers—they have much bigger feet. Hey, I'd say what we are is Chinese life partners!"

I did a double take. "What are you talking about? What are Chinese life partners?"

Kirk dipped his paddle and pulled expertly, deftly avoiding a clutch of rocks that loomed ahead.

"I just made that up. I don't know what the Chinese really call them. But when you save a Chinese person's life, then his life belongs to you forever."

A chill ran up my spine. "I've heard of that. But I thought it was American Indians."

He turned just as a cold spray of white water hit his handsome face, making it glisten. He looked sensational.

"Nah, I'm sure it was the Chinese. Well, we can find out, anyway. I'll ask my history teacher. He knows all that stuff."

"You really are sort of a nut, you know."

His white teeth flashed, setting off the sun-browned ruggedness of his face. "Why, thanks. I'll take that as a compliment."

"OK, but you'd better look out!" I shouted. "Rocks coming up on the right—"

We maneuvered carefully, gasping as we circled the gushing white sprays that shot up from the midriver boulders.

"Do you think this trip will ever end?" I asked wearily.

"I hope not. I'm glad I jumped into this thing with you, Abby."

I didn't like his serious tone. It made me uncomfortable. But I had to be polite.

"I'm glad you did, too," I said.

And I meant it.

Soon, of course, it was over, and we found that everyone had survived the trip. We all collapsed onshore when we reached the end of the run, where the buses were waiting for us.

"Abby! You're alive!" called out Suzi Browning. "How did you ever manage that raft all alone?"

"She had a partner." Kirk was standing beside me, tall and triumphant, smiling from ear to ear. And he had really cute ears, too, I noticed.

"*You?*" Suzi was incredulous. So was Jan, when she caught up with us.

"You saved Abby?" Suzi was staring at him as though he were a vision from heaven.

Then Kirk did an amazing thing: he put an arm around my shoulders in a most possessive way. "I told you, we saved each other. Partners."

The arm stayed there, and I was more aware of it than I had ever been of anything else in my whole life. I mean, I had on tons of clothes, and wet ones at that, but the sensation of that masculine hand and arm draped over me was like something burning right against my bare flesh.

Don't be weird, Abigail Morrell, I ordered myself. *Kirk is just—just what? Feeling glad to be alive? Feeling grateful because I happened along with a raft?*

He has a girlfriend, remember? Suddenly I did remember. Kirk Phillips was always with Colleen Kelly—always. She was a tall, stunning redhead, one of those who could easily have been a cheerleader except that she was too busy doing intellectual things. Running the newspaper. Serving on the student council. Getting into National Honor Society.

"Uh, where's Colleen?" I blurted out before I'd had time to think. After all, we were standing there as though we were going together, with my friends' eyes bugging right out of their heads. It was a peculiar situation, to say the least.

The question didn't faze Kirk a bit. "Colleen's home. She doesn't go for outdoor things like this."

"Well, I don't think *I* do, either," Suzie threw in, shivering in the cool afternoon air. "Not after this experience. Come on, let's get on that bus and back to camp. We all need dry clothes!"

I wondered how I could extricate myself from

Kirk's grasp. Finally I said, "Well, I had a good time, now that it's all over, and I thank you for everything." That was perfect. I pulled away, then took his right hand and shook it. Very platonic, very cool, and very levelheaded of me.

His brown eyes were twinkling with amusement. "I had a good time, too, Abby."

The handshake was quick and light. I didn't want any more electrical currents running between us, and we separated. He was whisked off by his crowd of friends, and I trudged along with Suzi and Jan behind the Brownings.

"My gosh, Abby." Jan spoke first. "What went on out there? The guy acts like he's your slave or something."

"Don't be silly. He's just kidding around. All we did was worry a lot and paddle and bail out and—just try to survive, that's all."

"That's all?" Suzi rolled her eyes heavenward. "Oh, wow, if only someone like Kirk Phillips would drop into my raft sometime! What a *hunk* he is, Abby."

I spoke dryly. "Maybe, but he's Colleen Kelly's hunk." The five of us picked up a raft and other gear to carry to the bus and the equipment trucks.

We were huffing and puffing along trails through the woods, dragging stuff that no human who had endured what we had should be expected to haul. Still, that was the law of river rafting. Nobody got pampered. We'd known that when we signed on.

"Did he say anything? I mean anything romantic?" That was Jan, staggering right behind me, half-swallowed up by the raft over her head. Jan was always searching for romance in books, in movies, and in real life.

"How could he say anything, Jan? We could hardly hear each other. You know how loud those rapids are."

But Kirk's voice was in my head, whispering to me. "You look awfully cute right now, Abby."

But cute? Who wanted to be cute?

At that moment I'd have given anything to be a tall, sophisticated redhead who was at home, polishing her nails and waiting for Kirk to phone.

Chapter Two

I wasn't at all like Jan, who was always dreaming about romance. I was going to be sixteen soon, and yet I'd never been in love.

I had a few friends who were boys, but no boyfriends. I think I wanted it that way; it seemed easier, somehow. No worries about dates and eye makeup and good-night kisses. I didn't want to fall for every good-looking or interesting boy who said hello to me.

So it shocked me when I found myself reacting to Kirk Phillips in the way that I had. Where was my inborn protection? Of all the boys in our whole town, Kirk was the very *last* person I should have flipped over. Because there was Colleen. And the fact that he was so popular at Brookdale High School while I was a nobody.

I know. We're never supposed to consider ourselves nobodies. I really don't, not in everyday situations. But when you're at a large high school and some kids are "in" and some are "out," it's easy to feel invisible.

Actually I've never minded being invisible. I've always kept busy in a lot of ways—baby-sitting, reading, writing plays. I've had my two puppet theaters, one for hand puppets and one for marionettes. I've made most of the puppets myself.

Kirk wasn't the first person to classify my looks as cute. My skin has stayed clear, and my light brown hair has its own soft, natural wave. Jan would kill for my hair, she often has said.

My eyes are hazel, although I've sometimes wished that they were a true brown—a dark, chocolaty brown like Kirk Phillips's. My figure is just fine if I stay on a semidiet. When I do pig out now and then, I immediately penalize myself with salads and skinless chicken for the rest of the week.

I certainly wasn't looking my best as we exhausted adventurers changed into dry clothes back at the Lehigh River Campground.

It was a typical camp—small wooden cabins in a circle and one big community house for cooking and eating. It was rustic, buried deep in the shade of tall pines and birches. The paths were thick with fallen leaves and pine needles.

Suzi, Jan, and I had a small cabin to ourselves

because there weren't that many girls on this trip. The Brownings were with another couple who were also chaperons.

We changed clothes in record time because we were beyond cold, we were frozen numb.

"How did we ever get into this, anyway?" Suzi was grumbling as she tried to run a comb through her wet blond hair.

"All your idea—remember?" Jan never let Suzi get away with a thing. "You saw the notice on the school bulletin board, and you were the one who said, 'Hey wouldn't that be fun? Something really different.' "

That was true. Suzi had spotted the notice put up by the town's outdoor club for a white-water rafting expedition in Pennsylvania. Since we lived in Connecticut, our parents were reluctant to let us go. They changed their minds only when Suzi managed to persuade her parents to go along as chaperons.

"Don't remind me." Suzi made a face in the small mirror she had set up near her bed. "We nearly got drowned, we could still come down with pneumonia, and besides all that, we *look* absolutely horrible. And with all these cute boys here!"

"Now there's our answer, Jan," I said, smiling. "That's why Suzi really wanted to go river rafting—because of the boys. We should have known."

"You should talk! You, of all people!" Suzi had whirled around to glare at me. "Who do you wind up with? Kirk Phillips, the most outstanding guy in our whole town!"

"She didn't exactly wind up with him, Sue." Jan sat back on her bed, enjoying the sparring. "I mean, there's still Colleen."

"You saw how he had his arm around Abby. Ve-ry possessive, I'd say."

If only she'd heard how he called us Chinese life partners, she would have gone right up the wall, I thought.

Suzi studied me with interest. "I suppose you're going to say you're not interested in him, Abby?"

I blushed. "I'd like to say that," I mumbled.

The dinner gong rang, and we quickly threw on turtleneck sweaters and jackets. We didn't want to miss a morsel, we were so starved. We ran, not walked, over to the community building.

"Dinner is *not* waiting for you," Mrs. Browning said with a mischievous grin. "You have to help make it—all of you."

"Guys, too?" The wail came from Joe Dalton, a big, sweet, and notoriously lazy boy who had probably never even roasted a hot dog in his life.

16

"Especially guys," Mr. Browning said fiercely. "This is a group effort. Whoever doesn't help doesn't eat."

So everyone, even the wise guys, helped to make supper. Naturally, I found myself teamed with—you guessed it—Kirk Phillips on the salad-making detail.

"Hi, again," he said, moving beside me as I was running some radishes under the cold water. I dropped about six radishes, and they clattered all over the sink.

"Hey, don't get all nervous." Kirk looked amused. Why did he have to be such a cheerful boy, as well as so darned good-looking?

"I'm not nervous," I declared as I bumped into a pile of lettuce heads and knocked them to the floor.

"Abby, relax, for pete's sake. I'm just here to help you with the salads. I'm an expert at this."

I looked up at him. "Are you an expert at everything?"

"No. Just salads and piloting river rafts and—oh, I'm great at slicing cold cuts, too." Seeing my puzzled expression, he explained. "I work in a deli part-time."

"I see. Well, I guess you'll be a lot of help then." I handed him a paring knife. "You can start with the cucumbers."

He stared at me. "Why don't you say, 'Start with the cucumbers, Kirk!'"

"What?"

"You've never said my name. I'd like to hear how you say it."

Flustered, I dropped all the radishes again. "You're being silly, you know—Kirk."

"Good." His voice was low and almost intimate. "You said that just fine. Now I'll do the cucumbers."

What was I to make of a boy like that? He'd been going with Colleen for so long that I thought of them as practically married, yet here he was, flirting with me like crazy. At least, that's how it seemed.

I thought of that expression, "When the cat's away the mice will play." And I wondered, *Is that the kind of disloyal boyfriend Kirk Phillips is?*

"How're you two coming along?" Mrs. Browning came over awhile later to check our work. "Why, that's just beautiful. I love the way you're doing those cucumbers, Kirk. So artistic."

And they were. He'd raked them with a fork so that they looked striped after he cut them. Very appealing, I had to admit.

"Well, hurry it up, kids," Mrs. B. urged. "Every person here is like a starving lunatic, and the hot dogs on the outdoor grill are almost done."

I chopped my lettuce and radishes faster, but I

was in slow motion compared to Kirk. He really was good. In no time we had completed two enormous bowls of crisp, colorful salad.

"Told you we make a good team, Abby." Kirk planted a kiss on my cheek. "I'm not being fresh, by the way. This is the way the Chinese compliment their life partners."

And, looking pleased and cheerful, he walked off, carrying one of the bowls of salad.

Jan marched over as soon as Kirk had departed. "I guess we can't leave you alone for a minute, Abigail."

"We are simply making salads, *Janet*," I said, trying to sound formal. She knew I hated being called Abigail.

"Salads, hah! I saw him kiss you. When are you going to tell us what's going on?"

I made myself very busy cleaning up the scraps of lettuce and other debris. "He—he's acting awfully funny, Jan," I finally admitted. "I mean, why would he be paying so much attention to me? I just don't understand—"

Jan stared at me. "You're very pretty, Abby. Did you ever think of that? And you have a terrific personality."

I groaned. "Colleen is pretty, Jan. What could he see in short, quiet me when he has that redhead who's a perfect ten?"

"I don't know," Jan said honestly. "It's a very

odd thing that's happening here. I'm sure that Kirk Phillips isn't the playboy type. At least, I'm pretty sure."

"He seems nice—sincere and friendly." I picked up the remaining salad bowl. "I think that's all there is to it. He's just being friendly."

We started toward the dining area, where kids were shouting, "Give us food! Give us food!"

"Just be careful, that's all," Jan added. "Somebody like Kirk could really break your heart."

I didn't need Jan to tell me that. My pulse had been racing ever since that quick, innocent kiss. My blood pressure had probably jumped a few points, too.

We sat down next to Suzi, who was flirting with a dark-haired boy from some other school. She didn't introduce him to us, but we didn't care. We were hungry.

Joe Dalton carried in several platters of hot dogs and looked very proud of himself. "First time I ever cooked," he told us, carefully setting down the food. "Guess I did a pretty good job, hmm?"

Kirk and several other boys were right behind him with rolls, onions, mustard, relish, and catsup.

We ate a quiet meal. After the food had been demolished, the Brownings and other chaperons made sure that the whole group helped to clean up.

"Now," Jan said wearily, "we can go and stretch out on our beds." Jan was tall and a bit on the chubby side and usually the first to suggest a little relaxation.

"Don't be silly," Suzi said, tossing back her blond hair. "We have a whole interesting evening ahead of us. That bunch from Roosevelt High School invited us over to their area for a camp fire."

"We don't even know them," Jan cautioned. "I don't feel like partying with guys we don't know."

"So come and party with *us*." We hadn't realized it, but Kirk Phillips and three of his pals were right behind us, standing on the steps of the community building. Kirk was wearing that big grin that I was coming to know so well.

A warning bell rang in my head. "I don't think so," I said quickly. "Jan and I are really tired, and I think she's got the right idea. We're going to get some sleep."

Joe Dalton, always the clown, wouldn't take no for an answer. "Don't be a party pooper, Abby. You either, Jan. We have a giant radio that can get all the best stations, even here in the wilderness. And we brought a cooler of soda."

Jan looked at me and shrugged. If I had said

no, that would have been enough for Jan. But, somehow, I couldn't say no. Maybe I was curious.

Or maybe I was just crazy.

So even Suzi abandoned her Roosevelt High guy and joined us at the boys' cabin. Since they had the soda, we contributed granola bars and the other munchies we had planned to save for the trip home.

We sat around listening to rock music and some Beatles classics, unwinding after the harrowing experiences we'd had that day. Suzi, for one, couldn't stop talking about her wild time being stranded on that rock.

"You can imagine how dreadful it was," she expounded to whomever would listen. "Especially seeing my poor parents out there in the river."

Kirk's eyes met mine. It was as though he was saying, "We know, don't we, Abby? We know what it feels like to be all alone out there, fighting for survival."

His eyes were mesmerizing me. I was fatigued and not thinking too clearly, but why did I have to react so strongly to him?

I couldn't stand it. I leaped up suddenly and ran outside to the fresh air.

Kirk followed me. We were all alone, with those

tall pines swaying overhead and the soft sound of the wind rustling through the branches.

"Something's bothering you, Abby," he said quietly.

"No," I lied. "Nothing's bothering me. Sometimes I just like to be alone."

He was silent for a moment. "You're sort of a loner most of the time, aren't you? At school, too, I think."

"I have friends," I said defensively. "I spend lots of time with Suzi and Jan and others."

"Is there any special guy, Abby?" he asked almost offhandedly, as though the answer didn't matter.

I looked down at the ground. I decided not to answer him. Ann Landers always says that a person does not have to answer personal questions.

"Why would you ask that, Kirk?" I asked very sweetly—just the way Ann Landers might have said it.

He chuckled. "Mysterious, aren't you? OK—I won't bug you with a lot of questions that are none of my business."

"Hey! What's going on out there?" demanded the loud voice of Joe Dalton through the open door of the cabin. "You two all right, or what?"

"We're just fine, Joe." Kirk was still chuckling. "Guess they think we need to be chaperoned."

I shivered. "It's pretty cold. I'm going back inside—"

"Abby." His firm tone stopped me cold. "I guess you don't know what to think of me. You probably think I'm some kind of rat who's looking to fool around, even though I go with Colleen. Am I right?"

"Well, uh—yes."

"It's not like that at all. I don't know if I can explain. I like you, Abby, but I'm not trying to come on to you—really, I'm not. Don't you believe that a girl and a guy can be friends—just friends, with no strings attached?"

"I—I'm not sure."

Kirk wouldn't speak until I looked right up at his face, which was partly visible in the dim light that came from someone's kerosene lantern.

"Well, that's how it can be, Abby. We can be friends—because of being Chinese life partners."

"Oh, you and that Chinese nonsense!"

He reached out and touched my hair, just for a moment. "It's not nonsense, Abby. You'll see. There's a bond between us. We'll be really good friends from now on."

"And Colleen won't mind a bit, I suppose?"

"Mmm, I don't think she will. She knows I'd never go out behind her back or hurt her in any way."

Then she's a lucky girl, I thought, and there

was a sudden, piercing stab in the region of my heart.

"OK, Chinese partner, you win." I forced myself to say it cheerfully. "We're friends from now on."

But I felt a chill, as though something eerie had just happened. *What am I getting into?* I thought. *How am I ever going to handle this?*

Chapter Three

Well, anyway, that should be the end of Kirk Phillips, I thought with relief when we headed home early the next morning in the Brownings' little Datsun. It had been an exciting weekend, in many ways, but I'd be glad to get back to Brookdale and my nice, sane, quiet life.

In spite of all the things Kirk had said, I knew that we had no business being "best friends." Not when I felt nervous just being in the same room with him!

"So now it's back to the old grind again," Suzi complained, staring morosely out the car window. "Nothing to look forward to except final exams and then the hot summer."

"What a pessimist you are," Jan told her, shaking her head. "You're sixteen already, so you'll probably find a job anytime now, whereas we—"

"We'll find jobs this summer, too, Jan," I interrupted. "I've *got* to. My family is going through a financial squeeze right now, and I really shouldn't have spent my baby-sitting money on this rafting trip."

Money had been tight since January, when my father announced that there would be almost no overtime work for a while for him. Lately my dad had even been reading the help wanted ads.

"You're right, Abby—we'll get jobs." Jan tried to sound positive. "Even if we have to manufacture our own, like walking people's dogs or something."

"So you had a good time river rafting, then?" my dad asked. I had arrived home about half an hour before, and my parents had sat with me while I had lunch. Now they were out working in the garden, while my little brother was napping. Our dog Mugsley was slurping at my face with enthusiasm as great as if I'd been gone for a year.

"We sure did," I said. "But I ought to tell you about the problems we had with our raft before you hear from someone else." I described our trouble, making it sound less serious than it really had been. And, of course, I glossed over the part about Kirk Phillips as quickly as I could.

"Who did you say the young man was?" my father asked. I should've known Dad would pick up on that. He's shrewd. "The boy who helped you to paddle your raft?"

"Um, Kirk Phillips. He goes to our school. He's—"

"Of course, I know the Phillips family." My father straightened up as though he had a crick in his back from too much yard work. "Richard Phillips was our lawyer when we bought this house."

"That was a long time ago, Ace," my mother reminded him.

Mom looked happy, in spite of being a bit concerned about my rafting adventure. She was wearing faded jeans and a youthful T-shirt, and her short brown hair was fluffy and cute, poking out from under a red cotton scarf.

Kirk Phillips, my mind kept repeating for no reason at all. I wanted, crazily, to say his name out loud, just to feel my lips shape the words carefully.

But, of course, I didn't. I smiled at my parents to reassure them that I was perfectly all right and hadn't come close to drowning in the Lehigh River.

"Well, it's good to have you back home again,

Abby," my father said, brushing some peat moss from the knees of his pants. Dad looked relaxed and rested, too, for a change.

In the past Dad had always worked weekends. In fact, we hardly ever saw him with all the overtime he had to work. So it was really nice to have him around, even if we were on a tight budget.

"So what's new here at home?" I asked, trying to escape from the fervent embrace of Mugsley.

"Oh," my mother said. "Mrs. Peterson called. Wanted to know whether you can baby-sit for the children during the summer while she's at work."

I groaned. "All summer? All day long? Aargh."

"I know what you mean," Mom commiserated. "Not much fun, hanging around someone's house every day, minding kids. But you'll be sixteen in a few weeks, Abb—I bet you'll find a job easily."

"Oh, I hope and pray. I mean, I love kids, but that sounds like too much." I was really glad my mother understood. A lot of other mothers would have said, "You have to think of the money, We really need the money—"

Which we did, I admitted. But I'd find some other way to earn a salary, I was sure of it.

In my room I plunked my suitcase on my bed

and gave one quick, approving glance around at my familiar collection of puppets.

"Hi, guys. Did you miss me?" I slipped my hand into the newest one, a shaggy, hand-puppet pup that I'd named Mugsley after my real dog. He was a soft golden brown, carefully sewn from fuzzy material that I'd found on sale at the fabric shop.

"I did a pretty neat job on you, Mugs, didn't I?" The puppet shook his head at me, wiggling with as much energy as my dog. I had used big brown buttons for eyes, and I'd embroidered his nose and mouth with red thread. He was one of my masterpieces.

"I'm going to write a play just for you," I said, putting him down and looking at some of the others I'd created. Among the hand puppets were a Mexican señorita, a Dutch girl, a boy from Italy, and an Eskimo boy. They were part of an ensemble I'd created about four or five years before, when I made up a United Nations sort of play after we had studied the U.N. in school.

Puppets were the only hobby I'd ever had, actually. I'd been making them since I was a very little girl, and I was good at it. There was a time when I'd almost given up the hobby, when I was about twelve. I'd thought that I was getting too old to play with puppets.

And then my parents had presented me with a

huge surprise—a baby brother named Stevie. Once we had a genuine, gurgling, lively baby of our own, I couldn't abandon the puppets. Stevie was always entertained by my little creatures.

Because my baby brother loved animals so much, I had created a regular zoo of hand puppets—a panda, a wise old owl, a pink elephant, an ostrich, even an anteater, among others. Most of the animals had cloth heads and bodies, whereas the people had heads made of papier-mâché, which I painted with gleaming enamels.

I'd made plenty of marionettes, too, with my dad's help. He'd provide me with the small pieces of soft wood for the body parts, and I'd make the heads with papier-mâché. I'd complete the marionettes by making tiny vests, skirts, blue jeans, or whatever seemed appropriate and comical. Adding the strings was the last part of the construction; I had to get them in just the right position—just the exact length from the control stick to the hands, legs, and head.

I was especially proud of a character I called Football Giraffe, made just for Stevie. Mrs. Marshmallow, a marionette who happened to have a wooden head, was one of Stevie's favorites, too.

I started to unpack. The sooner I could put away my suitcase, the sooner I could put the river-rafting weekend behind me. And then maybe I could forget that blond, brown-eyed boy whose face kept hammering away at my subconscious.

Why did Kirk Phillips have to be so unforgetable—and so unattainable?

"Abby!" The overjoyed little voice made me smile and stop my unpacking. There was Stevie, just up from his nap, still rubbing his eyes and looking sleepy. "You came home."

"Of course I did, sport!" I gathered him into my arms. My baby brother was three now, and still I never failed to be amazed at the miracle of him. I had been an only child for a dozen years, and then this wonderful human being had come along to brighten up our whole household.

"Did you go on the river?" he asked, staring at me with those big, green-brown eyes. I was sure he didn't know what it meant, going on the river.

"Yes, I did, and we had a lot of fun. Were you a good boy while I was away?"

"Yep. I wanted to play with Mrs. Marshmallow, but Mommy said no, so I didn't come in your room at all."

"I'm proud of you!" I planted a kiss on his damp forehead and reached behind him for Mrs. Marshmallow.

"Sure, and *I'm* proud of you, too, Stevie," I made Mrs. Marshmallow say in a completely different voice. She was plump and jolly and sounded Irish. I worked the strings so that she did a little dance.

Stevie rewarded her with a loud laugh. "I like the ones with strings," he declared.

With my other hand I reached for Mugsley. "Oh, you mean you don't like us hand puppets?" Mugsley had a deep, gruff voice and bounced his head up and down as he talked.

Stevie looked bewildered for a minute. And then put out his hand to pat the puppet dog. "No, I love you, too, Mugsley."

"I guess you just love all of us, then," Mrs. Marshmallow told him, settling the problem once and for all. "And now," I said in my own Abby voice, "why doesn't Stevie put on his sneakers, and we'll go outside with Mom and Dad?"

Stevie was happy to comply. I gave him another little hug when he was all zipped into his new red spring jacket.

Who needs a Chinese life partner? I thought. My life is just perfect the way it is.

But I wondered what it was that made my mind keep returning to the previous day's adventures with Kirk Phillips. Why couldn't I just forget the whole thing? Kirk was probably with Colleen Kelly, laughing and telling her about the narrow escape he'd had on the river.

I shook my head. I didn't want to think about that—about the two of them being together.

"Let's go, Stevie. We're going to play outside with the real Mugsley!" We laughed as we marched along together.

An hour later Kirk Phillips was on my front lawn with us, being kissed by that same real Mugsley.

He simply pulled up in an old rattletrap blue car and jumped out before I could squint to see who it was.

"Hi, Abby," he said cheerily. "So this is where you live."

"Who are you?" Stevie asked right away. He was enchanted, of course, the way little boys always are when they see someone tall and male. He stared at Kirk's sneakers in absolute awe. "You have big feet," he said enviously.

"Thanks, pal." Kirk's grin showed that he knew how to accept a compliment. "And who are you? Abby's brother?"

"Yes, this is Stevie. What on earth are you *doing* here?"

"Visiting with you." He smiled in the most maddening way. I noticed that his face was tanned from the day on the river and his brown eyes sparkled. He was wearing a brown sweater, big and woolly, that made his shoulders look broad. His well-worn jeans were faded to just the right shade of light blue.

I can't stand it, I was thinking. *Why is he here?*

"So who is this canine?" Kirk asked, shaking his head toward Mugsley, who was doing his best to topple Kirk.

"That's one of our Mugsleys," Stevie said matter-of-factly. Kirk looked both confused and amused.

"This one is the family pet," I explained. "His name is Mugsley. The other one is a puppet I made."

"No kidding? I'd like to see the puppet Mugsley."

"You want to see Mrs. Marshmallow, too?" Stevie asked excitedly. "Or Football Giraffe?"

"What have you got? A menagerie?" Kirk gave me one of those devastating smiles. My heart started to pound really fast. And that made me angry.

"Why are you here, Kirk?" I asked again. "Why aren't you with Colleen now? You haven't seen her all weekend."

"Colleen is busy with the yearbook committee this afternoon," he said, shrugging. "She invited them all over to talk about plans for next year's book."

"But—what about being with your family?"

"My parents are entertaining. A party for local political types. Our house is stuffed with stuffed shirts, to tell the truth."

"Oh." What could I say? He made it sound as though he didn't belong anywhere else in the world that particular afternoon. Could I say that he wasn't welcome in our house, either?

My parents came wandering around to the front of the house and looked surprised to see a boy there with us.

I had to do introductions. "Mom, Dad, this is Kirk Phillips. I might have mentioned him. He was on the river raft with me—"

"Of course you mentioned him, Abby," my father said, none too subtly. He put out a hand to Kirk. "Glad to meet you, Kirk. I understand you saved our daughter's life."

"I'm happy to know you, too," my mother said quietly. She was appraising Kirk in a thoughtful way. My mother is a good judge of character; maybe it comes from all the psychology she's studied at the local college. I had a feeling she was impressed with Kirk.

Stevie pulled on my jacket. "Go get the puppets, Abby," he reminded me. "Kerp wants to see them."

We all laughed. "Not Kerp, Stevie. His name is Kirk."

"I like Kerp better." Stevie's big eyes filled with tears; he was humiliated because he had been laughed at by four big people. We should have known better.

"I think Kerp sounds better, too," Kirk assured him, giving Stevie's shoulders a man-to-man thump. "Maybe you could name one of the puppets Kerp."

I began to think I was going crazy. Kirk Phillips, the handsome and popular upperclassman, was standing on my front lawn discussing puppets with my three-year-old brother.

I had no choice but to go upstairs and get the puppets. If my parents thought there was anything out of the ordinary about this visit, they didn't show it. When I got back, they were conversing with Kirk just as though he were any other friend of mine, like Suzi or Jan.

I was shy about showing the puppets. They were my babies, after all. What if he thought they were stupid?

But he was astounded. "These are really *good*, Abby. You made them? I can hardly believe it! Look at the detail on this string marionette—"

"She's Mrs. Marshmallow. She can talk, you know!" Stevie announced.

Kirk turned to stare at me in admiration. "Don't tell me. You're a ventriloquist, too?"

"No," I admitted. "I hide behind a curtain when I work the puppets, so nobody sees me or the way my lips move."

"But Abby's great at voices," my father piped in. "Each little character has its own special voice—and personality. And Abby writes plays for them, too."

"Dad," I groaned, hoping he'd stop bragging about me. "Kirk doesn't want to hear about—"

"Yes, I do." Kirk spoke firmly as he examined the football giraffe with care, moving its little helmet as though it were something very precious. "I think this is terrific. Where do you perform these plays?"

"Oh, nowhere," I said quickly. "This is just my hobby."

"You have to be kidding." Kirk stared at me. "You could probably make a fortune with these little things. Puppet shows are popular, you know, with little kids."

"I suppose so, but I've never wanted to—" I began. But I stopped to think. Maybe I should listen to him. Maybe he was saying something that made sense. Wasn't I looking for a way to earn money this summer?

"Where's your stage?" Kirk asked excitedly.

"In the garage. There are two of them, one for hand puppets and one for marionettes. But—"

"Can I see them?" Kirk turned politely to my parents. "Does anybody mind?"

My mother looked highly amused. "Of course not. You two run along and do—whatever. We'll take Stevie with us to the backyard."

"No, I want to stay with *Kerp*," Stevie howled as they carted him away. "I want to see the stage, too!"

Fired by some of Kirk's enthusiasm, I led him to the garage. Inside were my two handmade stages, lovingly crafted by my father years before and neatly wrapped in huge plastic bags.

Kirk looked them over. "They're nice," he said. "But maybe not bright enough. Or flashy enough. We need really colorful theaters to impress people when you're on the stage."

"Do you really think anyone actually would—would pay me to put on my puppet acts?"

"Are your plays any good?"

I blushed, then said simply, "Yes, I think they are. I studied a lot of plays, and then I developed my own style of writing. I think I have decent plots and—"

"That's good. You need lots of action, too." His face lit up. "If you don't mind my butting in, Abby, I know we can get you rolling toward some real money."

"You sound so convincing," I said.

"Absolutely. I'm going to help you get some publicity, and the orders will come piling in. So maybe the first thing is to get these theaters painted. Can we do it now?"

"Right now?" I was startled.

"Why not? I have nothing on for what's left of this afternoon. Do you?"

I stared up into his brown eyes. I wanted to go ahead with the project—for money's sake—but I knew, deep down, that having Kirk around was just going to lead to heartbreak. Or heartburn, or whatever it is when a girl falls for a boy she simply cannot have.

Get out of my life, I wanted to scream. *Get out now, while my heart is still in one piece.* But I didn't.

Chapter Four

For the next two hours, Kirk and I painted. He insisted on a bright blue—his favorite color—for the hand-puppet theater. And we found some rich, glossy, off-white paint for the marionette theater. We decided we'd embellish it with some fancy scrollwork later.

It was weird, working side by side with Kirk. Nothing like this had ever happened to me, but I couldn't relax and enjoy it—not when he was Colleen's boyfriend.

I tried not to think about how sweet he was. I told myself that what mattered was that we were accomplishing something important. Even my dad, when he came ambling by to see what we were up to, thought we were doing terrifically.

"The stages look wonderful, all spruced up like that," he said sincerely. "And the idea of doing shows for money—why didn't we ever think of that before? You're going to be a hit, Abby."

Dad wandered off again, and I said, "Why are you doing this, Kirk?"

"I told you a million times. We're friends now."

"Oh, yeah. Chinese life partners."

"That's right." He finished touching up a corner of the blue theater. "It's not a problem, is it, Abby?"

"Well, it's—it's peculiar. Not as though we've been friends all our lives or anything."

"So? We're friends now. That's what counts. Might as well make the most of what we have now."

"But what do you—" I hesitated. "What do you get for all your troubles? I don't see—"

He turned toward me. "I don't have to get anything, Abby. I told you this before. Didn't you ever hear of doing something with no strings attached?"

I groaned. "Is that a pun? Because of all my string puppets?"

"Maybe. Hey, this looks terrific now, don't you think? Now are you going to do a sample play for me?"

"Oh—I've never performed for anyone except the kids in the neighborhood, and my family, and once for Jan. I don't think—"

"Will you listen to yourself?" He sounded

almost angry. "Here we are, working our heads off so that you can perform for audiences—and you've decided to be shy. You can't have it both ways, Abigail Morrell."

"Don't call me Abigail," I blurted out.

"I will call you Abigail unless you listen to me. Shyness is all very cute and fine, but not when you're going into show business. We've got to get you revved up. You're going to have a busy time from now on."

I did one of my marionette plays, *Mrs. Marshmallow Goes to the Football Game,* and we let Stevie come back to watch it with Kirk. Both of them roared. Kirk said he was laughing because the gags were funny enough to amuse older people, and Stevie, we knew, was just hysterical because he enjoyed seeing Mrs. Marshmallow and Football Giraffe doing lots of loud, silly things.

"Very good," Kirk pronouced. "Really. You have to learn to speak louder, I think, so your voice will project to a large audience, but—"

"I can work on that," I said. I was really enthused about this whole idea. Maybe, deep down, I had always wanted to perform before an audience but had never had the courage. Now I had the feeling that it was really going to happen.

Kirk looked at his watch. "I've got to get

home," he said. "I'll let you know what I come up with."

"Wait. What do you mean?" I called out, but he was already striding across the lawn toward his car.

"Bye, Stevie. Bye, Abby." He waved and took off.

"I like Kerp," Stevie said happily, taking my hand.

"I do, too," I said automatically. "But I don't know, Stevie. I don't know if this friendship is a good idea."

"Abby? I have something to tell you." Jan's voice coming over the telephone sounded very unlike her. Instead of her usual joking manner, she was almost subdued.

"What's going on, Jan?"

She took a deep breath before she told her news. "I think that Joe Dalton likes me!"

I smiled. "Jan, that's really great. He's such a nice person. When did all this happen?"

"I think at the campground, when we had that party in their cabin. We were talking a lot, and he was telling me how he goes to a health club for workouts—you know, exercise machines and all that. And just now he called me! He invited me to go as his guest next weekend, to try it out for myself."

"That sounds wonderful. Maybe you'll both get skinny together." Both Jan and Joe were slightly chubby, but usually Jan wasn't sensitive about the subject.

"Maybe we will," she answered blithely. I was happy for her. Jan had been hoping for a romance for years. She'd been reading romance stories ever since she was twelve.

"Um—I have something to tell you, too," I ventured.

"Yes?"

"I had a visitor this afternoon. Kirk Phillips."

There was a dead silence for a minute. Then, "You're kidding, aren't you, Abby?"

"I'm afraid not. He just came over unexpectedly because—because he said that Colleen was busy with her yearbook staff and his parents were giving a party, and—"

"But, Abby, this is getting serious. What in the world does he want?"

"He wants to be my friend, he says. Oh, Jan, I don't know. He went crazy over my puppets and started making plans to get me into show business. As a way to earn some money."

Silence again. Then, "Well, that's the first thing that's made any sense, at least. It's a great idea. Is there any way I can help?"

"I'm not really sure. I suppose I might need help if I actually get any jobs. Some of the plays

I've written would be better if they had music along with them."

"Aha! I could work the record player for you. Or tape player, or whatever you decide on."

"It wouldn't be so frightening if you came along, Jan," I said honestly. "And maybe we can split the money, sometimes."

"Tell me, what did your parents think of Kirk being there?"

"Oh, they really liked him. So did Stevie, of course. Dad thought Kirk was great, painting the puppet theaters the way he did. And naturally they're grateful to him for helping me on the raft ride."

"I don't know, Abby. This whole thing is pretty weird. But if he just wants to be friends, then what the heck?"

"I hardly know how to have a boy for a friend," I mused.

"And I hardly know how to have a boy for a boyfriend!" Jan was bubbling over with enthusiasm. "I keep wondering if Joe Dalton means this health club thing as a real date, or is he just trying to recruit a new member?"

"I guess you'll find out soon enough." I didn't want to discourage Jan, but Joe Dalton didn't seem like a very romantic character to me. He was such a big, loud clown.

But then, people can change, or so my mother was always telling me.

I wondered what Mom would have to say on the subject of Kirk and his very strange behavior.

"You seemed rather ill at ease with that Phillips boy, Abby" was what she said when we were all sitting down to a late Sunday supper.

"Did I?" I took a knife and started cutting up some chicken on Stevie's plate.

"I don't mean to pry, dear, but you know, you don't have to be embarrassed just because a boy shows interest in you. You're almost sixteen. You're old enough to date if you want to."

Oh, if only it were that simple!

"I might as well explain something to you, Mom—and Dad." I sighed deeply. "Kirk Phillips is not interested in me in that way. He's been going with a girl in his class for a long time."

My mother frowned. "That's odd. I could have sworn that he was very interested in you, Abby. Are you sure about this?"

"Positive. They're the golden couple at school—Kirk and Colleen. They even look golden, with his blond hair and her long, beautiful red hair."

Stevie got excited because he'd heard Kirk's name. "I like Kerp. He has big feet, Daddy."

My father took a spoonful of cranberry jelly. "What does 'going with a girl' mean, anyway? They're not engaged or anything?"

I sighed again. "No, not engaged. But at Brookdale High, when a couple's been going together that long, it almost seems like an engagement. At least a preliminary one."

"You remember, Ace," my mother reminded Dad. "I used to wear your class ring and that ID bracelet you bought for me, and nobody else would ever ask me out."

"I remember." Dad was obviously thinking the whole thing over. "Doesn't seem as though Kirk Phillips is too loyal to this Colleen, however."

I repeated the statement for what seemed the millionth time. "Kirk and I are just friends, Dad. Just good friends, because of the way we helped save each other's lives. Dramatic events tend to pull people together."

"Hmmph." That was the last Dad had to say on the topic. He was much more interested in his mashed potatoes and gravy, anyway.

But the wheels were turning in my mother's head, I could tell. Sooner or later she'd give me her psychological evaluation of this matter. I'd just have to be patient and wait.

For the time being, Mom flashed me a reassuring smile. "Well, whether Kirk is just a friend—or whatever—he does have a great idea about your going public with the puppets."

I nodded. "Mmm, I'm starting to think so, too. Jan offered to help sometimes. I'm going to call Mrs. Peterson and tell her that I can't baby-sit this summer. I'll be working on a new career."

"I have a good feeling about this, Abby," Mom said in a quiet voice. "There are no other puppeteers in Brookdale, as far as we know. I do think the time is right for puppet shows. And yours have always been so lively."

"Thanks, Mom. I do appreciate your confidence."

"Don't sound so surprised! I've seen your plays, and they can be very professional. Of course, you've always been a little bit shy, Abby, so you'll have to combat that."

"Oh, that's no problem." I tried to laugh it off. "Don't forget, I'll always be behind the curtain. No one ever sees the puppeteer."

"I wouldn't be so sure about that, Abby," Mom said. "There might be times—"

"Don't scare the girl," my father said. "Let her take one step at a time."

"One step at a time," Stevie parroted, smiling gleefully. "One step at a time, Abby!"

Chapter Five

I always walked to school with Jan and Suzi, and Monday morning was no exception.

They were both giving me lectures about Kirk. "Don't be hurt, Abby, if he's forgotten all about you by this morning," Suzi warned me. "I mean, he's so popular, you know? And maybe he was just bored this weekend, so he popped over to your house. But when Colleen finds out what he's been up to—" She made a slitting motion across her throat with her hand.

"You're probably right," I agreed. "But actually it doesn't matter because I can do the puppet stuff myself, now that he's gotten me all enthused. Jan's going to help with music, and we should be able to run things quite well."

We were trudging up the shortcut path to

school, trying not to get our legs scratched by grass and weeds that were too long.

"Abby, I'm glad I found you!" Suddenly, amazingly, there was Kirk Phillips trotting toward us, waving some papers in his hands. He was a beautiful sight for Monday morning. He was dressed in a blazingly white shirt and a pair of navy slacks that emphasized his long legs. His big brown eyes were lit with excitement.

He said hi and smiled politely at Suzi and Jan, then turned to me. "Abby, do you have a minute? I have some flyers to show you."

"Flyers?" I was bewildered again by this boy.

Kirk produced a packet of papers. "Yes, I worked on these last night for a while. We have to come up with a name for your puppet act, and a logo—you know, a special way of printing the name. He showed me one of his artistic renditions. "How's this—Abby and Company?"

Suzi poked her nose in. "Hey, that's cute. Look at the drawing he did of you, Abby. It looks like you, peering out from behind the puppet stage. That would be wonderful publicity."

Kirk said, "If you OK it, Abby, I can get them printed up. Then all of us can distribute these all over town. You two will help, won't you, Jan and Suzi?"

Suzi looked up at Kirk's handsome face, and you could almost see her melting. Ordinarily

Suzi didn't do favors for anyone, even Jan or me, her best friends.

"Of course we will," she said, gushing. "I'd be *glad* to help with a project like this, Kirk."

"Great! So what do you think, Abby? Do you like the name, or did you have something else in mind?"

"I don't know," I said slowly. "I never thought of a name before. Couldn't we use something that left the Abby out of it? Like maybe The Mugsley Puppet Troupe?"

"There she goes again," complained Jan. "Always shy and modest. It's your puppet show, Abby. Why not make people aware of who you are? How about Abby and Friends?"

Kirk and Suzi nodded. "That sounds even better. More friendly. Little kids will love it!"

I looked over at the flyer that Kirk handed me. "You're a good artist, Kirk," I said. I couldn't believe that he'd gone to all this trouble for me. And I knew that my friends were impressed beyond words. He had printed, in a neat calligraphy style, "Local Puppet Show for Hire. Children's Parties Our Specialty. No Job Too Small or Too Large."

"Do we have to have this drawing of me, though, Kirk?" I really felt embarrassed by the attention. "After all, nobody sees me behind the curtain."

"I'll take it out if you really prefer, Abby. But you're not going to be hiding behind that curtain forever. We're going to be using photos, too, you know."

I glared up at him. "I suppose you're an expert photographer, too?" I couldn't help sounding sarcastic. But he just laughed.

"Expert artist, expert photographer, and, as I've already demonstrated, a whiz at making salads and saving river rafts. There's no end to my talents."

Jan was studying the well-drawn flyer over my shoulder. "What are you planning to major in at college, Kirk?" she asked.

His animated face became blank. "Oh, college. I'm programmed to study law, just like my brothers and my father."

"Programmed?" The three of us stared at him because of the cynical way he'd said that.

But he brushed it off. "Forget it. Cancel that last statement. I'm going to be a lawyer, Jan." He pulled the flyer out of my hands. "OK, I'll get to work on these as soon as I can. And, Abby, you just get ready for a very busy summer."

He disappeared as quickly as he'd appeared.

"Well, for heaven's sakes," Suzi whispered, almost in awe. "He really is your friend, Abby."

Jan put a steadying hand on my shoulder. She

knew how attracted I was to Kirk Phillips and how confusing all this was for me.

Suzi couldn't resist saying just one more thing. "I just wonder what Colleen's going to think about Kirk's cozy new friendship."

"All right, people," called our gym teacher, Mr. Parker. "Set your ball down on the tee, the way I showed you and then see if you can master the grip. Like so—"

Poor Mr. Parker. He was always trying to get us interested in odd sports. He expected to see a whole field full of enthusiastic pupils, and nobody cared in the least. Almost every kid at Brookdale High had a severe case of spring fever and was joyful just to be outdoors and away from stuffy, hot classrooms.

Except me. I had something else to be concerned about. I had forgotten that Colleen Kelly was in this gym class. It hadn't mattered before; she'd been just another junior girl who'd never noticed me. But now, with Suzi's ominous words still ringing in my head, I was worried.

Colleen looked elegant, as always, even in her gym shorts and her gold sports shirt. She'd pulled her long hair back into a neat ponytail for gym class. She was looking at Mr. Parker with great concentration, as though it were very important for her to master the game of golf.

Maybe golf was something that would look good on her college applications.

I tried not to get nervous about Colleen. After all, none of what had happened over the weekend had been my fault. I had never chased after Kirk; I had never encouraged him in the least. And I'd tell her that, too, if she ever started to give me any trouble.

"Pssst. Abby—"

Oh, no. It was Colleen, moving toward me with that golf club firmly gripped in her hands. I winced. One slice from a tall girl like that, and I'd be in Concussion City.

"Uh, hi, Colleen," I said and wondered if my voice trembled.

"Hi." She had a clear, no-nonsense voice that made her sound much older than a high-school girl. "Kirk showed me those posters he drew for your puppets."

"Did he?"

I looked at her face to see if she seemed angry or anything. She didn't. She looked interested.

"I think the whole thing is an excellent enterprise." Colleen seemed so sincere that it almost knocked me over.

"You—you think so?"

"Yes, absolutely. And if there's anything I can do, I'd like to help. I'm going to mention your puppet business to all the people on Marwick

Hill, where I live. They give lots of birthday parties up there for children."

Marwick Hill, I thought. The fanciest section of Brookdale. "That's really nice of you, Colleen," I managed to say.

She smiled brightly. She certainly was pretty, with her very white skin and that soft red hair framing her face. No wonder Kirk was so crazy about her. And that made my heart ache, just a tiny little bit.

"I think it's a fun project," she said. "This town needs a good puppeteer. Good luck, Abby. I'd better get back to golf."

I stood there with my head swimming. This encounter was even more peculiar than anything else that had happened so far. Why was Kirk's girlfriend suddenly being so friendly toward me? Had Kirk told her everything? About the raft rescue, and the Chinese life partner stuff, about his visiting my house on Sunday afternoon?

"Miss Morrell, are you going to get started with your golf swing or not?" the teacher called out, looking severely wounded.

"Here I go, Mr. Parker," I answered.

But my mind was on Colleen. I wondered if I had just hallucinated. If not, that meant that Colleen was now my friend, too.

Kirk Phillips, what are you doing to me? I

wondered. I took a wild swing at my golf ball, and this time I didn't miss.

Instead, I struck the side of the ball—what Mr. Parker would call a "slice"—and the next thing I knew there was a loud thud against the roof of a nearby Volkswagen.

Then I heard a loud groan from Joe Dalton, our class comedian. "Do you realize whose car that is? None other than Mr. Parker's!"

The entire class went into hysterics, clapping for me as though I were a heroine. Mr. Parker looked as though he were about to have a coronary because there was now a tiny dent in his car roof.

"Ah, that car is a rusted old tin can, anyway," Joe reminded me.

But I felt like a prize klutz. And there was Colleen, tall and perfect in every way, swinging with precision at her golf ball.

Things got even more complicated that afternoon after school. Jan had walked home with me because she wanted to take another look at my puppets and the newly painted theaters.

We were puttering around in my garage, with Stevie right on hand to give us his opinion about everything.

"Mrs. Marshmallow is the funniest one," he

was telling Jan. "But sometimes Football Giraffe is better. Kerp likes the football one."

We smiled and ignored him, as usual. We didn't pay attention when he announced, "Here comes Kerp. In the blue car. And the other guy, too."

"Sure, sure, Stevie," I said, not looking up from the script I was showing Jan. "I was thinking of stadium music of some kind for this show, Jan. Some sort of football march. Can you think of one?"

Jan knew a lot about music. "I'll come up with something," she promised. "And in the meantime, have you thought about making a cheerleader puppet? That might fit in really well with this scene—"

"Hello, ladies." We heard the loud voice of Joe Dalton and almost jumped out of our skins.

"I told you Kerp was here!" Stevie said with pride.

"Hi, Abby." Kirk Phillips had the most radiant smile I'd ever seen. "Have I got news for you!"

I was tongue-tied. I couldn't believe that he was here again. "Wh-what?" I stammered.

"A job, Abby. A birthday party job for Thursday of this week. Are you ready for it?"

I just stared at him. It was Jan who said, "That's fabulous news, Kirk. How'd you manage that?"

"I took the flyers to the printer's office, and the woman who works in there took one look and said, 'I wonder if she would come to my daughter's birthday party? Is it expensive?' " Kirk was grinning like a little kid.

"And you said—" prompted Jan.

"I said, 'Ms. Morrell will probably do the job for very little money, as this is her first performance.' We need this one to get started, Abby. After this one, we'll have lots of publicity. So what do you say?"

I felt my heart thumping in my chest. "I guess—I guess we'll go for it," I said bravely.

"Of course you will, Abby!" Jan seemed very pleased. "And now, what do we do to get ready?"

All of us looked at Kirk. Somehow he had become the leader of this project, even though I was supposed to be the puppeteer.

"Well, that's why I brought Joe with me," Kirk said. "Joe knows a lot about lighting. He's worked with the community theater as lighting man and electrician, and he has a few ideas about lighting the puppet stages."

"Lighting them? I never thought of that," I whispered.

"You're in good hands, Abby. Fear not." Joe Dalton was talking to me, but in actuality he was stealing looks at Jan and almost blushing. *Why, I think he does like Jan,* I thought, surprised.

And, of course, anyone could see that the feeling was mutual.

Then it hit me. What a perfect foursome we would have been—if only it weren't for the small matter of Kirk Phillips's being someone else's steady.

The boys began to work, planning and making notes, studying the stages and angles, talking about volts and watts and other technical things.

"Do you think we need all this for a birthday party?" I asked.

"Maybe not," Kirk said. "But later, when you get into bigger audiences, you'll need lots of lighting. So we might as well get it squared away now."

"Will it cost Abby a fortune?" Jan asked, coming right to the point as she usually did.

"Nah." Joe looked slightly sheepish. "I'm going to lend her some old equipment from the community theater—at least for a while. After she gets rich, she can buy some lamps and things of her own."

Jan smiled at him. "That's really very helpful of you, Joe."

Joe grinned in his usual way. "I know. I'm just a big, softhearted slob. What can I say?"

"Well, I can say thank you," I told Joe. But he was still looking shyly at Jan.

Ah, sweet romance, I thought and turned away to see what Kirk was doing to the stage floor of the marionette theater.

"We might need a little backdrop here, Abby," he said. "For that scene in the football stadium, you know? Maybe something that looks like the crowd in the background."

I stared at Kirk's profile while he was busy setting up small pieces of cardboard and explaining his idea. What a terrific profile it was! His lashes were long. His nose was straight and perfectly sculptured. And he always seemed to be smiling, no matter what he was talking about.

He turned those brown eyes on me, and I wondered if he knew how I'd been staring. But he didn't seem to notice anything unusual.

"I hope you don't think I'm butting in too much, Abby. I just keep getting these brainstorms, and I can't help wanting to come over here to tell you."

"I don't mind," I said quietly. My heart had skipped a beat or two.

"Good. Then I'll keep on being a pest." He winked. "So we can tell Mrs. Smith that you can do the show?"

"I can do it," I said, making up my mind that I *would* be ready by Thursday.

"We have to get going, Joe," Kirk said suddenly. "I have to be at work at the deli by four today."

"I tell you what," Joe said. "You go ahead. I'll stay here with the girls for a while, and then I'll walk home later."

"Oh?" Kirk frowned, looking confused for a moment. Then the truth seemed to dawn on him. He looked at Jan and Joe and grinned with real pleasure. Then he handed me a piece of paper.

"That's Mrs. Smith's phone number, Abby. You'll have to call her and finalize the arrangements about the party. I suggest that you make the fee really low—OK? She doesn't seem to have much money."

"Fine," I said. "And—thank you, Kirk."

He looked at me in an odd way. "You're welcome, little partner." Then he hurried off toward his car.

Chapter Six

"Welcome, ladies and gentlemen," announced Jan, who was dressed as a bright, raggedy clown, "to the birthday party of Miss Jordan Smith. You're in for a real treat today because you'll be seeing a performance of the best marionettes in town—Abby and Friends!"

Jan was really hamming it up, I thought, and I admired her stage personality. As for myself, I was a basket case. I was sure that my voice wouldn't work at all. I was sure that the whole thing would be a series of mistakes.

"Just relax, Abby," my friends had told me earlier as we'd set up the elaborate marionette stage in the Smiths' living room. Joe Dalton was wielding his lights from across the room, and Kirk was there with his camera. Every time I blinked an eye, he was snapping a picture.

Suddenly I realized that Jan had finished her introduction, and I was on. Taking a deep breath, I began to work the wooden controller that held the strings for Mrs. Marshmallow.

And, surprise, my voice *did* work! It came out loud and clear. I had done Mrs. Marshmallow so often for Stevie, and in rehearsal, that speaking in her voice was like second nature to me. And working the strings was, as usual, pure magic for me.

I always feel very much in control when I work those strings. I move a finger, and the marionette's foot moves. I tip the control stick, and she walks across the stage or she dances. Or, in the case of this particular play, Mrs. Marshmallow went running. She was chasing her runaway kitten and unknowingly stumbled into a football stadium.

The children laughed when I had the ticket taker yell out, "Hey, lady! You can't go in there! You have to buy a ticket to go to a football game." Mrs. Marshmallow, however, didn't pay any attention to him. She was too busy trying to catch her kitten.

The laughter of the kids really gave me a boost. My play was all right. They were enjoying it! All along I'd been worried about the football game comedy. But here was proof: an audience full of children was really laughing good and loud!

So, riding on a puppeteer's high, I acted out the little drama. My voice never faltered. Jan played the football music at all the right moments. Joe kept the spotlight on whichever puppet was doing the talking.

And Kirk kept snapping pictures—the mad photographer let loose at a children's party.

It's going very well, I told myself, and my voice became even louder and more full of confidence. When I brought out my newest string puppet, the cheerleader waving her pom-poms, the kids whooped with recognition and delight.

I felt gratified. I'd worked all week getting her constructed and painted exactly right.

My puppets moved and spoke almost with a will of their own. It happens that way sometimes; they take over, and I become just the instrument to give them life. It's a strange sensation, but a nice one, because the play goes along automatically and without any errors.

Finally after Mrs. Marshmallow had disrupted the entire football game and found her missing kitten, the police escorted her from the stadium and the play was over.

The kids clapped and cheered wildly. I saw Kirk cheering wildly, too, and I smiled, wondering why that boy was so full of pure, childlike joy.

"Abby, that was wonderful," Mrs. Smith said right away. She stepped forward to urge me to come out from behind the curtain. "Wasn't she marvelous, children?"

There was a lot of applause. "Please take a bow, Abby," Mrs. Smith begged. "The kids would love to meet you."

I had no choice. My face, no doubt, was fiery crimson, but I smiled pleasantly and held up Mrs. Marshmallow so they could see just how she worked, controller and all. I found it hard to speak in my own voice so I let Mrs. Marshmallow, with her Irish brogue, explain how the strings moved her body parts.

The kids wanted to come closer to ask questions and see behind the stage. I let them do so, knowing this would always be one of the fascinations of any puppet show. Finally, I had to use my own Abby voice to tell exactly how I had constructed each character.

And Kirk went on snapping pictures of everything I did.

"I think everything went perfectly," Jan said as we packed all the equipment into Kirk's car.

"Mrs. Smith was so pleased that she gave me a big bonus check," I told them. "So I'd like to share the money with you guys."

"No way," Joe said. "I had too much fun. Anyway, I have a job at Harvey's Service Station. I don't need money, Abby."

"Me, neither." Kirk was carefully stashing the large stage into the trunk so that he wouldn't crush anything. "Looks like we're going to need a van someday, Abby. This stuff isn't going to transport so well in a car forever."

Jan said, "Abby, you can't give any of us any money. But I'll tell you what. You can buy us something to eat, if you want."

I grinned. "You're on. What would you all like? Pizza? Big Macs? Banana splits?"

"Would you mind if we went someplace nonfattening?" Jan looked sideways at Joe. "I'm sort of on a diet."

"Hey, there's a great salad bar at the deli where I work. Maxl's, in the mall." Kirk lifted the box of marionettes with great care, knowing how tangled the strings could get if the box fell. "Want to go there?"

"Good idea," Joe said. "I think I'll have salad, too. I'm supposed to be on a diet for my health club. They like to force people to get on the scale every week or so."

So we went to Maxl's, which was more of a good-sized restaurant than just a delicatessen. It smelled great, like pickles and salami and all kinds of cheeses. The decor was sort of like a chalet with dark beams and shelves full of drinking mugs and steins.

And this was almost like being on a double

date, I thought as we all helped ourselves to huge bowls from the salad bar. Kirk went to pour coffee and diet sodas for everyone because the deli was busy, and Maxl, the owner, seemed grateful to have Kirk's help behind the counter.

Joe said loudly, "Is this Maxl's deli? Where you fill your belly?" and the customers all laughed.

It was a lot of fun. We were all in a good mood after the success at the birthday party, and we did a lot of laughing and kidding around. Joe, of course, was always a riot, anyway, with one joke after another. He had Jan giggling so hard she could hardly swallow her lettuce or alfalfa sprouts.

Kirk was somewhat quieter. He sat back in his chair, giving the impression of being quite relaxed, but I could see that his mind was going a mile a minute. And he often seemed to be staring at me.

"I guess you're on your way now, Abby," he said at one point, just as we were finishing up our salads.

"You mean with the puppets? Yes," I answered. "And all because of you, Kirk." I couldn't help looking at him with real admiration.

"Not really." There was an expression in his deep brown eyes that I couldn't figure out. "You are one talented performer, as we all saw this afternoon."

"Too right," Joe agreed with an outrageous English cockney accent.

"And you really don't need us," Kirk went on. "But I hope you'll let us keep on helping whenever we can, at least for a while."

"Oh, yes, Abby," Jan echoed. "It was so much fun, being a part of it."

"None of it would have happened at all if it hadn't been for Kirk." I chose my words carefully. "And Joe's lighting and Jan's music made everything so much more professional. So why do you say that I really don't need you? I *loved* having you guys there."

"Hear, hear," Joe howled, raising his glass of Tab. "Let's drink a toast to the finest bunch of puppeteers in the East!"

We all smiled, except Kirk; he was still looking very solemn and thoughtful. But he raised his paper coffee cup along with the rest of us, and we clinked our toast in a silly, happy-hearted gesture.

"This day will go down in history!" Joe proclaimed.

I felt tears, for no apparent reason, starting to fill my eyes. "Thank you, guys," I said. "I really think you're great. All of you."

And that's when Maxl came over to find out what all the celebrating was about. The stout, elderly gentleman ended up sitting down with us and raising his own coffee cup in a salute.

"Good luck to Abby," he said in his thick German accent. "If you are a friend of Kirk's, then I know you must be a fine young lady."

Chapter Seven

Spring was in full bloom and turning quickly into summer. The forsythia bushes had long since burst into gold, and lilacs had blossomed into fat, sweet-smelling clusters of purple and white. With the weather so warm, going to school those last few weeks really was a chore.

"Well, I've got a job," Suzi announced one afternoon as we sat sunning ourselves on the patio around her pool. "I'm going to wait on tables at the Frankfurter Shop."

"That's great, Suze," Jan said. "And I think I'm in at the day-care center for the summer. My mom put in a good word for me there. She says I'm effective with little kids."

I angled my face so that it would catch a few more rays, and stretched out my legs. "I'm happy for both of you. I just wish my sixteenth birthday would hurry up and get here before it's too late to apply for anything."

"Oh, Abby, you don't have to worry about a job," Jan said quickly. "You're going to make plenty of money with your puppets."

"Maybe," I said not too confidently. "And maybe not. Those flyers that Kirk made have been hanging up all over town, but the phone hasn't exactly been ringing off the wall."

"Give it time," Suzi said. "Hmm. By the way, isn't today the day the Brookdale weekly paper comes out?"

"Why, yes," Jan answered as if on cue. "And what do you know? I just happen to have a copy of it right here."

Suspicious, I turned to stare at them. "OK, what's going on?"

Jan pulled out the newspaper with a dramatic gesture and opened it to the middle. "And here's Abby!" she crooned.

I stared. I couldn't believe my eyes. Right on page six, in a huge, four-column spread, was a picture of *me*. It had been taken by Kirk, of course, and it showed the little kids at the birthday party crowding around me and the puppet theater, with Mrs. Marshmallow prominent in the front of the picture.

"Puppeteer Captivates Young Audience," the headline shouted. There was a story, too, which carried the by-line: Kirk Phillips. It told a lot about me, but even more about the great experience the show had been for all the children at Jordan Smith's party. Kirk used quotes from the children and even from Mrs. Smith.

"When did he do all this?" I asked, shaking my head in amazement. "I didn't know he'd sent anything to the newspaper."

"He's full of surprises, that guy," said Suzi as she sloshed some sunscreen across her nose.

"Kirk wanted to make this a surprise," Jan told me. "Didn't he do a great job? He's just as good a writer as he is an artist."

"And photographer, too," I said grudgingly. I was embarrassed at this publicity. Suzi would have lapped it up in a minute. But to a very private person, it felt just awful to be splattered on the pages of the newspaper.

Still, I knew I had to go along with it. Publicity would be the key to becoming a professional puppeteer.

That night our home telephone did start ringing.

First it was the children's librarian at the Brookdale Public Library. The library was planning an English festival for one day in the summer. Was I able to do a Punch and Judy hand puppet show, by any chance? I told her yes, I could research it and come up with something.

Then, in quick succession, there were two calls from mothers who were looking for something special for their children's birthday parties. One lady wanted the marionette show, exactly as shown in the paper, and the other wondered if I could do both hand puppets and the string puppets. I said yes to both of them.

"You'll have to start keeping a little appointment book," my mother advised, then handed me a blank notebook like the ones she used for her college courses. "Might as well take that one, Abby. I won't be needing it this summer."

"Why not, Mom? You always go to summer classes."

My mother sort of shrugged. "Not enough money this year for tuition. But I don't mind, really. It'll give me more time to spend with you and Stevie."

I didn't like the sound of that. Was our money situation really getting that bad? Dad had always declared that even if we had to eat cheese casserole all week long, he wanted to see Mom getting the education that meant so much to her.

Mom put a hand on my head. "Don't worry about things, Abby. We'll manage, I'm sure. And now that you're getting both rich and famous, we'll soon be living in the lap of luxury."

I grinned. "Yeah, sure, rich and famous. But Kirk did do a wonderful job on this publicity, didn't he?"

Mom was silent for a moment. "Kirk seems to be very good at everything he does, I'd say."

"True." I opened the notebook and started making entries. "June 3, birthday party at 5, Marwick Hill, Madden family. June 10 . . ."

Mom cleared her throat. "Kirk was here this afternoon, Abby, while you were over at Suzi's house."

"He was?" I looked at my mother in surprise.

"Yes, and he spent about half an hour playing with Stevie. Promised to take him fishing one of these days."

I frowned. Kirk had been here, and I had been out sunning my face somewhere else. Oh, well. Maybe it was for the best. The less I saw of Kirk Phillips, the less I'd have these fantasies about him.

Mom was staring at me, and I knew that it was time for her opinion to be aired. I'd been waiting for this. My mother, the Dr. Joyce Brothers of Brookdale.

I tried to outguess her. "You're going to tell me that I should discourage Kirk from coming here so often, aren't you, Mom?"

"No, I wasn't going to say that at all. I think he's a fine young man."

"But you do realize—I explained to you that he's going with someone else."

"Yes. But I'm not terribly convinced of that, Abby."

"You're not? Well, I am! And I just hate this, getting to like him more and more and knowing that he's never going to be available."

"Never is a strong word, Abby." Mom smiled, a mysterious Mona Lisa smile. "I see Kirk Phillips as a boy who's going through some sort of transition in his life right now. And you seem to be a part of it, Abby. You and the puppets—and yes, even Stevie."

"A transition? What in the world is that supposed to mean, Sigmund Freud?" I loved to tease her about her psychology jargon.

"I can't say yet." The Mona Lisa smile was still in evidence. "I imagine that Kirk is not sure yet. But it will all become clear eventually."

The phone rang again, and I hoped it might be another puppet show job. But before I picked it up, I said, "You're not a psychologist, Mom. You're trying to be a fortune-teller. I think you ought to get yourself a crystal ball."

Still smiling, Mom disappeared while I answered the phone. It was Jan, calling to tell me that she had lost a whole two pounds already.

The next morning I found Kirk in a maple tree near the school parking lot, taking photos of a bird's nest. I said hello to his feet.

"Oh, Abby." The muffled voice came from up in the leaves. "Wait." Pretty soon he came sliding down, looking somewhat rumpled but exhilarated.

"Good morning," he said. "I know I'm a mess, but I do this sometimes. Then I go inside to clean up and change my shirt before classes start."

"I didn't realize you were so serious about your photography," I commented.

Kirk wiped some perspiration from his face with a clean handkerchief. "Now you know. If I could, I'd go to art school instead of college. But that kind of talk is heresy at my house."

"Why? You're so good at drawing and photography."

"My folks don't approve," he said, and the subject was closed. "So how are you this morning?" He looked straight at me, and I felt my knees getting kind of wobbly.

Stop it, Abby, I ordered myself.

"I'm fine. And pretty grateful," I said. "I want to thank you for sending that story to the newspaper and to tell you that it brought me three job offers last night."

"Did it? I'm so glad. I'm not such a bad PR man, am I?"

"PR? Oh, you mean public relations. You're terrific, Kirk, and you must know it. I don't know how you managed all that."

"Nothing to it. I went to see the editor with the photos, and he thought it was so cute that he asked me to write the story. I was counting on that; I took some notes at the party. I liked doing it."

The sunshine was gleaming on his beautiful light hair, and I had an overwhelming urge to reach out and touch it. Instead, I moved a few feet away from him, hugging my books tightly to my chest.

"I think it's great that the puppet show dream is coming true for you, Abby."

For an odd moment I didn't care at all about the puppets. All I could think was that Kirk and I were alone. It felt almost like being a couple.

Then I looked down at my shoes and sternly reminded myself that I was being a prize jerk again. Kirk was my friend, and that was all. Absolutely all.

"Hey, I've got to get inside," I said quickly. "I have to—uh—see my English teacher about an assignment." It was a lie, but I just had to get away from Kirk. "Thank you for everything, Kirk. I'll see you later."

"What's the big hurry?" Kirk called out, sounding a little hurt. But I pretended I didn't hear him and just kept rushing off toward the school.

"Let me warn you—don't get the tuna salad," Jan whispered to me in the lunch line that day. "Yecch. Ugh. Too much mayonnaise."

"Thanks," I said as she walked back to the table where she was sitting with Suzi. I chose a ham sandwich and a salad, then joined them.

"We want to talk to you, Abby," Suzi said as soon as I'd sat down with them. "Now I want you to listen, and I don't want you to say no like you always do. It's time you had an open mind, Abby, about boys and dates and—"

"What is she talking about?" I turned to Jan, hoping for a direct answer.

Jan said, "It's this, Abby. We want to fix you up with a date. Now don't say no! He's a nice boy, a friend of Joe's, and his name is Scott, and—"

"I won't say no." I spoke quietly.

"What?" gasped Suzi.

"Are you serious?" Jan seemed stunned. "Do you mean it, Abby? You'll go on a blind date with Scott Boardman?"

I shook a little salt on my salad. "I'll go."

"Just like that? No questions asked?" Suzi looked as though she might be about to have heart failure or something.

"No questions asked. If you say he's somebody nice, then I'll give him a try."

"I cannot believe this," Jan murmured. "I simply cannot believe this. But I'm so glad. Maybe we can have some real fun together."

"Maybe," I said morosely. I speared a boring-looking slice of cucumber. And that reminded me of Kirk and the fancy way he fixed cucumbers.

I'll go on this date with whoever-he-is, I thought grimly, *because I can't just keep drifting and caring so much about Kirk Phillips. I really need to know some other boys.*

Chapter Eight

My first date. *Big deal*, I thought. I'd be sixteen the next day, and this would be my first date. I chose an apple-green cotton dress because I liked to imagine that some shades of green made my hazel eyes look better. I used the curling iron on my hair, so I had a shoulder-length tumble of soft brown curls. *Big deal*, I thought as I looked in the mirror.

Jan had been pretty vague about where we were going for this great occasion, and I didn't really care, anyway. The important thing was that I was making the effort.

"You look really nice," Jan told me when she and Joe and Scott arrived for me at about seven o'clock on Saturday night.

"You sure do, Abby." Joe, though he was crazy about Jan, seemed to like me. Why couldn't I be as comfortable around Kirk as I was near Joe? "I want you to meet my friend Scott Boardman," Joe went on. "Scott goes to Clarke." Clarke was a private school in our area. "He's my next-door neighbor and one of my best friends."

"I'm glad to meet you, Scott," I said quickly so things wouldn't become awkward. I could tell right away that Scott was the shy type.

"Hi, Abby." Scott had a nice smile. He was not terribly tall—next to Joe Dalton he looked like a midget—but since I'm short, too, that didn't matter. Scott also had a nice face. Nothing memorable, but he was pleasant-looking, and well-dressed in a suit and tie. His layered hair was sort of sandy, and his eyes were a clear, honest blue.

In short, Scott Boardman seemed like a perfectly OK boy. But he wasn't Kirk Phillips.

And that was the kind of thinking, I told myself, that I'd have to stop.

Scott met my parents, and all the polite things were said, and then we were on our way. I still didn't know where. I asked, but everybody seemed to be conspiring not to tell me. So I just sat, determined to relax in the backseat with Scott. He was asking me about my puppets, and I was answering him and trying to think of questions to ask him.

"Oh, nuts," Joe said as he was driving along

Main Street. "I forgot something at my house. Do you guys mind if I run home for it?"

"What did you forget?" Jan asked in a teasing way. "Your calorie counter?" They were helping each other with their diets and were being quite successful so far. They had gone to the health club to work out several times, too.

When we reached Joe's house, it looked sort of dark. "Why don't you come in for a minute?" he invited. "I have a new record I want to play for you."

I became suspicious. I thought this was turning into one of those times when the parents weren't home and the boys wanted to get us alone. But I followed everyone in, anyway, just to give Joe the benefit of the doubt. The four of us stepped into the small front hallway of his house, and suddenly a blaze of lights came on.

"Surprise!" called out a chorus of voices. "Surprise, Abby. Happy sixteenth birthday!!"

I was speechless. I had never expected anything like this. I looked around and saw, besides Mr. and Mrs. Dalton, Suzi and her newest boyfriend, Al, and two other couples who were friends from school. There were balloons and paper hats, and a tableful of food with a big birthday cake in the middle.

"We've been planning this for weeks," Suzi

said, pinning a corsage of white roses on my dress. "Happy birthday, Abby."

"But this is so lovely," I said, overwhelmed. "And here, at Joe's house. Whatever made you think of such a thing?"

Joe started his teasing. "Oh, we were just looking for an excuse to have a party, actually. So we decided to use your birthday. Don't get all flattered, Abby."

I grinned. "OK, I won't."

"And now—how about some music?" demanded Jan. She went over to the stacks of albums and started selecting dance records. Joe's parents smiled at all of us and announced that they'd be upstairs, watching TV in their bedroom. But they'd look in on us every so often, they warned.

It was a nice party. Once I got over the initial shock of having a surprise party thrown just for me, I enjoyed myself. Scott was a polite, attentive date, and he wasn't a bad dance partner. I was able to follow him with no trouble.

It's probably more comfortable to dance with short guys, I mused, trying to think positively. No doubt it would be ludicrous trying to dance with someone as tall as Kirk Phillips. No, this was definitely a good thing, being out with Scott.

When Scott pulled me a little bit closer, for a

dance number that was slow, I didn't protest. Might as well give this experiment my one hundred percent cooperation, I thought. I'd never danced with a boy before. And I'd never been kissed. Maybe before the night was over, that would also change.

Then the door bell rang, someone opened the door, and in came Kirk and Colleen. Instantly I felt as though I'd been kicked in the stomach—hard.

"Hey. We heard there's a birthday celebration going on here," Kirk called out, his usual cheerful voice carrying loud and clear. "So we came to give the birthday girl sixteen whacks."

"None of that, none of that," Joe told him, laughing. "But I'm glad you two could make it. Hi, Colleen."

"Are you all right, Abby?" Scott asked. "You look so pale suddenly. You're not sick, are you?"

I tried to smile. "No. Maybe I just need a few minutes break from dancing. Mind if we sit down, Scott?"

"You sit," he said with great concern. "I'll go get you a glass of water." He plunked me down on the couch.

"Happy birthday, Abby." Colleen sat down beside me, her eyes sparkling with good wishes. "I'll bet you were surprised."

"Yes," I said. "It's—it's so nice you could come."

"Oh, Kirk wouldn't have missed this for anything. He's always talking about how you're his Chinese life partner and all that."

"I'd have thought he would have forgotten about that by now," I said, staring down at my lap.

"Kirk? No." Colleen chuckled softly. She reminded me of a woman who's been married for so many decades that she knows her man thoroughly. I tried not to sigh.

Scott returned with my glass of water. "I don't believe we've ever met," Kirk said, striding over to take Scott's hand for a handshake. "My name's Kirk Phillips."

Shyly Scott introduced himself.

"You're here with Abby?" Kirk questioned, looking at me and then back at Scott.

"Oh, Kirk, stop acting like a big brother," Colleen scolded. "How about dancing with me? Or did we come here just to eat birthday cake?"

The next hour or so was pure torture for me. I danced with Scott, mostly, and once with Joe, just as a joke—a jitterbug sort of dance. Kirk didn't ask me for a dance, and I was glad.

I think I was glad. I didn't want any more complications. I was trying hard to enjoy the company of Scott Boardman, a perfectly nice boy, but somehow it was impossible.

I was relieved when Kirk and Colleen finally left, and I was just as happy when the party broke up at about midnight. I was getting a slight headache by then from forcing my smiles.

Joe drove us home, and Scott held my hand all the way during the ride. But he was too shy to give me a kiss.

Chapter Nine

My real birthday, the next day, was a quiet one. My grandparents drove up from New Rochelle and took us all out to dinner. We dined at the Hammond Lake Inn, which is right on the shore of the lake and features a buffet that can really turn you into a blimp.

"You're not eating much, Abby," my grandfather observed as he got up to go back for seconds on the prime ribs.

"I guess I'm not so hungry, Poppa."

He smiled knowingly. "You must be in love then. Is that it, chickadee? You're in love?"

"No. Absolutely not!" I said much too forcefully. And then to cover up, I shrugged. "Oh, what the heck. I guess I'll go for some more Swedish meatballs."

So it's come to this, I thought. *Now I have to*

stuff myself in order to hide my emotions from relatives.

This was what Kirk Phillips was doing to my life—not to mention my waistline.

On Monday after school my mom drove me to the Department of Motor Vehicles to get my driver's permit. Mom and Dad had decided that, with all these puppet jobs coming my way, I'd need my license. I couldn't depend on Dad and my friends to transport the puppets forever.

While we were waiting in the unbelievably long line at Motor Vehicles, Mom told me that she had taken a midnight-to-eight job as a nurse's aide at Brookdale Hospital. She'd be starting the following week.

Years before, Mom had been a nurse's aide, but she'd never been too crazy about bedpans or back rubs or changing sheets. She loved working with people, she always said, but she felt better suited to working with their minds and their emotions.

"It's just a temporary job, Abby, probably. Until things start to get better for Dad at Kromden. Or maybe I'll love being a nurse's aide again and make a career of it. Whoops!" She went running after Stevie, who must have thought it would be fun to slip behind the long counter to see the Motor Vehicle Department's computers.

When she returned, with a grumpy Stevie in tow, I said, "Oh, Mom, that's just awful. You were so excited about becoming a psychologist. You've got to find a way to get back to college."

"Don't worry, I will." She gave Stevie a quick kiss to soothe his hurt feelings. "I don't give up on my dreams that easily."

"I'll take care of Stevie for you in the mornings," I said. "So you can get some sleep. And then maybe I can get an afternoon or evening job, after Dad is home to baby-sit."

"That'd be all right, hon. But don't forget about your puppet shows. You've got a career started there, too, and it's part of your dream."

Her words were very comforting. *That's absolutely right*, I thought. *I am a puppeteer and possibly on my way to becoming a successful one!*

I don't have to sit around thinking about some boy who'll never be interested in me. I have something better to do.

I took finals that week, cramming, worrying, and in the end, doing just fine on most of them. Then school was out for the summer.

"No more pencils, no more books," Jan sang on the last day. Jan was unusually happy these days, in spite of being on a diet. It didn't seem to bother her at all to skip pizzas, or milkshakes, or even french fries.

She was in love. It was that simple. And I envied her.

Anyway, school was out for two whole months, and, oh, the freedom of it! That first day I slept sinfully late. When I finally got up, I cleaned my room thoroughly. I had to organize a lot of my puppet supplies, especially the scraps of cloth and other materials for constructing new puppets.

I was doing research on Punch and Judy for the library's English festival. They'd be hand puppets, and Punch had to look like a real rogue. Big nose, hunched back, thick red lips, and a stick in his hands. During the course of the show, he'd yell at his dog, his wife, his friend the doctor, and would even throw his baby out the window.

I shrugged. I never did like Punch and Judy shows. But if that's what they wanted, I'd get to work right away with papier-mâché and make Punch's ghastly little head.

"Can I help you, Abby?" Stevie asked, peering into my room as I was gathering things together to take out to the garage, where I did my papier-mâché work. He loved working with the sloppy paste and water and paper strips. He was always in heaven when I made a puppet.

"Sure, you can help. You can make a puppet of your own, Stevie. How would that be?"

"Good." He padded into the room, looking adorable in his denim overalls and Muppets T-shirt. "Can I make a Kerp puppet?"

"You, too?" I said softly. It seemed as though everyone was conspiring to keep Kirk Phillips on my mind.

We went out to the garage. Making the puppet's head was the most tedious part of the construction, but I'd been doing it for so long that it was second nature.

I'd blow up balloons to the size of the heads and paste newspaper strips all over them— except for the neck area. Later I'd pop the balloons and have perfect hollow puppet heads.

I started making four heads at the same time; I'd need Punch, his poor wife, Judy, the dog, and the doctor. For the baby I'd use just a little bundle of cloth, like a doll.

"Well, you sure look busy," a familiar voice said from behind me. "Both of you."

"Kerp!" Stevie called out. "Hi, Kerp. I'm making a Punch puppet with Abby."

"So I see. It looks very nice, too." Kirk stood there, almost insolent, as though daring me to say my usual, "Why are you here?" So I didn't say it. Instead I smiled pleasantly and asked him how his photos had turned out.

"Pretty good. I'm improving all the time, I think. I've decided to turn over some of my candid shots to Colleen for the yearbook next year."

I hated it when he mentioned Colleen. But I said, "That's great. I guess she's grateful to have a boyfriend who's a photographer."

"Are you kidding?" He laughed as though I'd said something monumentally funny.

"I don't understand."

"I told you, I love to do art projects—draw and sketch and take photos. My secret ambition is to be a professional photographer. But to Colleen, that's like saying I want to be a punk rock star."

I stared at him, sensing that he was serious. "You mean it, don't you? Really? A photographer, instead of a lawyer?"

"Yeah. Anything, instead of a lawyer. A restaurant chef, an artist, a novelist, a wedding photographer—maybe even a puppeteer's manager."

I frowned. "I never know whether you're kidding or not. If you feel so strongly about not being a lawyer, why don't you tell your family?"

He leaned down to watch me work. "I've already told them. It didn't go over too well."

"But no one can *force* you to become a lawyer if you don't want to be one."

Kirk sighed. The shadow of sadness that crossed his face made him look even more handsome—if that was possible—and very young and vulnerable. My heart went out to him.

"In the Phillips family, the Phillipses' sons do what Father Phillips tells them," he said almost as though repeating a litany. "And now I don't want to talk about that. Tell me what's going on with the puppet industry?"

I discussed my ideas for the Punch and Judy show, and Kirk turned to the stage, figuring out how to embellish it so that it would look more ornate.

Kirk started drawing up plans for gold curtains and intricate decorations for the top of the stage.

"This is what you really love, isn't it?" I ventured. It was fascinating to watch him when he got excited about an idea. "You like doing things with your hands instead of your brain, I think."

"Sometimes. That's why I really don't want to go to a regular four-year college. But when I mention art school, it turns into World War Three at my house."

I reflected for a moment. "I can understand how you must feel, Kirk, but not to go to college at all—that would be foolish, wouldn't it? I mean you're so smart, and your folks have the money.

You ought to get as much education as possible. Then later you can make your decisions."

"Hah. Now you sound like Colleen."

I felt put down. But that was puzzling. Colleen was the girl that he loved, after all.

"My puppet head is done," Stevie told us proudly, and we admired it. It was a pasty, blobby, solid ball of paper, and a puppet head should, of course, be hollow to allow for fingers. But Stevie would never know the difference. The next day when it was dry, he would paint it and the accomplishment would make him happy.

Kirk suddenly said, "So, anyway, I never did wish you an official happy birthday."

"Of course you did. You were at my surprise party."

"But I didn't wish you a special happy birthday."

I stared at him. "You aren't going to deliver those sixteen whacks, if that's what you think," I said firmly.

He pulled a small box out of his pocket. "Do you have a charm bracelet?" he asked.

"Why—no—I—"

He handed me the pink-wrapped box. "Well, maybe you can wear this around your neck then."

My fingers were trembling as I opened the package. Stevie was tugging at my leg, excited because there was a birthday present being opened.

Inside, sitting on a bed of soft cotton, was a perfect little miniature string puppet—and it was in gold.

"You know I can't accept this, Kirk," I managed to say.

"Oh, give me a break. Of course you can."

"But, Kirk, it's so expensive. And so very lovely." I held it up to the light to examine the tiny details of the marionette.

"I can afford it. I work long hours at the deli."

I stamped my foot. "Kirk, no, I can't let you do this. And, besides, what about Colleen? She wouldn't like the idea."

"My dear Chinese life partner, it was Colleen who helped me pick it out. So what do you think about that?"

I didn't know what to think. And I certainly didn't know what to say, except a feeble "thank you."

Kirk walked around the garage, trying to look casual. "So, Abby, who was this Scott guy you were with the other night?"

"Oh, a blind date. He's a friend of Joe's."

Kirk pretended to flick at a spider he saw crawling. "So—you two seemed to be getting along really well."

I gave him a quick sideways glance. "I guess

we did." Then I laughed. "Listen to you. If you don't mind my saying so, you sound like a prosecuting attorney right now, Mr. Phillips."

Kirk laughed, too. "I suppose I do. Just ignore me when I get nosy."

"I intend to." I turned back to my puppet making.

He stood there watching for a few minutes. "You know what, Abby? You're a lot of fun. I like the way you kid around. Your family's like that, isn't it?"

"I suppose so. Dad always says if you can't have money, you might as well have laughs."

"That's pretty good. And you Morrells have dreams, too. Your mother told me about wanting to finish college. And you with your puppets—" He stopped for a moment. "In my house everybody is dull and serious. Studious. No laughs at all."

I couldn't think of a reply to that. It sounded so very sad.

"So now you know one of the reasons why I like to come over here. Even Colleen's house is dull. Her mother and father are both lawyers."

Then Kirk and Colleen had a great deal in common, I was thinking. No wonder they'd been drawn to each other.

"Well, thanks for the lovely birthday present," I

said to change the subject. "I'll wear it on a gold chain, and I'll always treasure it."

"Hey, now that you're sixteen, you'll be needing driving lessons. Let me know if I can take you driving sometime."

I think we'd better not, I answered silently. I was terrified at the idea of spending so many hours alone with my "no-strings" friend.

"Maybe, sometime," I said. "Right now I'm going to be looking for a part-time job."

He looked startled. "Really? In addition to the puppet shows?"

"Yep. I need steady money. Things are getting so tight that even my mom took a job."

"Oh." Now it was Kirk's turn to look startled. "If I can help in any way—"

I slapped some more paper strips on Punch's head. "You can let me know if you hear of any job openings, I guess."

"I will."

Just then my mother called out from the back door. "Abby? Telephone for you. It's Scott."

That was a surprise.

"I suppose that's my cue to leave," Kirk said, sounding grumpy all of a sudden. "Wouldn't want to keep you from your wonderful new love."

If only he knew, I thought. But I grabbed

Stevie and said, "Let's go inside now, Champ. Abby has to answer the telephone."

Kirk's face looked almost grim as he said goodbye.

Chapter Ten

Scott invited me out to see a movie, any night that I chose. I decided that it was essential for me to accept. I had just spent all that time with my so-called life partner, and I was in a state of real turmoil. I looked down at the tiny gold marionette charm. How much could a girl stand, after all?

So we settled on Friday night; we'd make it a double date with Jan and Joe. Maybe if I saw enough of Scott, Kirk would get the idea and stay away.

Though somehow I doubted it. If his home life was dry and humorless, he was just looking for somewhere to hang out where people liked to laugh. Oh, well.

"Look at Abby's birthday present, Mommy," Stevie was blabbing. Mom wanted to see it.

"Beautiful," she pronounced, lifting the tiny charm out of its box. She'd been trying on her new work uniform, a white two-piece outfit. She looked trim and efficient, ready for a long night's work on Two South, the surgical recovery floor where she'd been assigned.

"Your uniform looks nice, Mom," I said. "Hey, I finished working on the puppet heads for now, until they dry. You wouldn't feel like taking me for a driving lesson, would you?"

Mom raised her eyebrows thoughtfully. "We'd have to take Stevie along. But, sure, why not? I have a few errands to run in town, and you two can stop for ice cream, if you like, while I shop."

Mom changed clothes, and Stevie and I cleaned the paste from our fingers. Then I drove very carefully into downtown Brookdale. It was scary, getting the feel of the road and the traffic and also figuring out just how the car handled. But it was exciting to be mastering a new skill. I felt very adult.

I parked near the Village Green, so Mom could go to the dry cleaner and the post office. I walked with Stevie over to the library, to talk to the children's librarian about the Festival. She seemed very pleased with my research into Punch and Judy.

"Now can we get an ice-cream cone?" Stevie begged. It was a hot day, so I didn't blame him.

As we were walking toward our old favorite, the Chocolate Shop, we passed a sign on a storefront that read, "New Ice-Cream Shop Coming soon. Watch for Our Grand Opening."

A little bell rang in my brain.

I knocked on the shop's closed door, and finally a pleasant, middle-aged woman came to answer it.

"We're not open yet, dear," she said.

"I know. But I'm here with a business proposition," I said quickly before I could lose my courage. "My name is Abby Morrell, and I have a puppet show for hire. I wonder—would you be interested in having a sidewalk show performed on your grand opening day?"

She stared at me, and I thought she was going to tell me that I was pretty nervy. But she said, "You're the girl in the newspaper. The one who does the birthday parties, aren't you?"

I smiled. "That's me," I said cheerfully. "And I could set up a stage right out front, if you like the idea, and try to draw customers to your new store."

The woman nodded her head. "I love the idea. You're hired, Abby. Can you be here on Saturday morning, bright and early?"

"Sure I can. All you have to do is tell me which kind of puppets you prefer, hand puppets or marionettes. Maybe I can write a special play.

About a little band of animals who each want a different flavor of ice cream?"

We talked for a few minutes more and decided that I'd bring the puppets over for her to see one day during the week. We shook hands on the deal, which made me feel like a real business-woman. And I walked away from there feeling ten feet tall.

I had made a deal, all on my own! Even though it had been Kirk who'd gotten me the publicity in the first place, this transaction had been completed by Abby Morrell, all by herself. It was a terrific boost to my morale.

And then, not ten feet away from the ice-cream shop, I ran into Colleen Kelly. She was dressed in a summery gray suit, with an elegant silk blouse, and was wearing stockings and high heels. She looked like a career woman, at least twenty-five years old.

"Hi, Abby," she said warmly. "What a cute little boy. Is he your brother?"

She was working, she explained, at her parents' law office right there on the Village Green. She'd been helping around the office for so many years that she knew as much as any legal secretary, so they always hired her for the summer.

I was impressed. And I was also deflated, somehow. Even though I loved my puppet career, it seemed awfully childish compared to

108

Colleen's job in the real world of lawyers. I couldn't even imagine dressing up every day as Colleen was, much less handling important problems for clients.

"This is my coffee break time. Would you like to go to a sandwich shop with me?" Colleen asked. I almost choked.

"Uh, I'd like to, but I have to meet my mother in five minutes," I said. "I'm having my first driving lessons today."

"Ah, yes, that's always a challenge." Colleen spoke with the grown-up air of one who has been driving for years. Again I felt young, and short, and insignificant. "Oh, Abby, you haven't said. Do you like the charm we bought?"

I wasn't going to mention it. But now that she had, I said, "Yes, of course. I really love it. Thank you, Colleen."

"Oh, you're welcome. You know, Abby, I'm glad to see Kirk getting interested in your puppets like this. It sort of gives him something else to think about, besides photography."

I stared at her. "You don't approve of his being artistic?"

"It's not that, exactly," she said softly. "I honestly don't think Kirk is serious about wanting art school; it's just a form of rebellion against his family. A way of trying to get out of college. And I don't want to see him make a mistake he'll regret later. He's too smart not to get an education."

But what about an education in art? I wondered. The whole discussion made me sad. Didn't poor Kirk have any say in the matter? It sounded as though everyone was ganging up on him.

"Don't forget ice cream," Stevie whined, tugging at my arm.

"Oh, yes, we've got to run, Colleen. I promised Stevie a cone before we meet Mom."

We said goodbye and parted. I wished that I hadn't run into her. As nice as Colleen was, she certainly had put a damper on my day.

"You're sure you don't want any popcorn?" Scott asked Joe and Jan just before the movie began.

"No, thanks," they both said regretfully, and Jan pulled two apples from a small paper bag she had in her purse. Being in love was a great motivating force. Jan looked absolutely terrific already. She had a tan from working outdoors at the day care center, and her clothes were starting to get big on her. Even her hair had a brighter sheen to it.

"Well, it's just you and me with this popcorn," Scott told me. I dug in. I could afford a few extra calories. I'd been working really hard all week, gluing and shaping and dressing puppets and helping Mom organize the household before she had to start her hospital job.

The movie date with Scott Boardman was not romantic. Scott was basically shy and had little to say about himself, so he was always asking me about the puppets as though I were a big show-biz personality. If it weren't for Joe and his loud, crazy jokes, the whole evening would have fallen flat.

After the movie we went to Jan's house and took a walk around the block—three times. Jan and Joe wanted to get their mandatory exercise. They both wore jogging shoes and moved with a lot of energy, while Scott and I plodded along, wondering just when the marathon was going to end.

The only good thing about that whole night was that we didn't run into Kirk and Colleen anywhere.

I tried to care about Scott. I really did. When he walked me home, finally he kept an arm around my shoulders, but very timidly. And at my door I began to get the feeling that the time for a kiss had finally come.

But I chickened out. "Gosh, I'm tired," I said quickly, pulling away from him and pretending to yawn. "Those two superathletes can really wear a person out, can't they?"

Scott smiled. "Maybe we can go out sometime without them, Abby," he said hopefully.

"Maybe." I didn't know what to do about Scott. He was so nice that it didn't seem fair to keep him dangling. But my heart belonged to someone else.

Yet I had to make myself forget that someone else. "Listen," I said impulsively. "Suzi has been talking about giving a party in the middle of the summer. She's calling it her Summer Dream Ball. If you'd like to go to that—"

"I'd love to. It sounds pretty fancy."

"It might be. She's talking about formal dresses and all that. Suzi dreams of being a debutante, I think. Well, anyway, good night, Scott."

My conscience was clear. I'd extended an invitation to him. So that let me off the hook, didn't it? I didn't have to let him kiss me.

Still smiling innocently, I opened my door and slipped inside.

Chapter Eleven

Balloons and music and crepe paper streamers surrounded Abby and Friends on Saturday as we did our first sidewalk puppet show alone.

I had set up my blue puppet stage right outside the entrance to the new ice-cream shop. Jan couldn't be there to work the music, so I had a little tape recorder that I worked whenever necessary.

The sun beat down that whole day, which wilted me but was great for the ice-cream business.

Lots of people stopped in front of my show, and I pulled out all my tricks. Mugsley, the puppy, wanted a strawberry ice-cream cone, and he kept making promises to his mother, a new, larger dog puppet that I'd made in a hurry.

"I'll clean my room, Mama," Mugsley said

maybe sixty times that day. "If only I can have a cone at the Ice-Cream Shoppe . . ."

I used all my other animal hand puppets as well. They talked about their preferences for vanilla, strawberry swirl, or chocolate marshmallow. The little kids loved the act. And parents didn't seem to mind stopping, because a puppet show on the sidewalk isn't something you see every day.

It was a long and tiring day, but I felt really important. Each time a family went into the store for ice cream, I knew I'd been a pretty good salesperson.

The MacDonalds, who were the store owners, gave me a great big bonus check when five o'clock arrived. "You were wonderful, Abby. You really drew attention to our place!"

Happy though exhausted, I began to pack away my puppets.

"Do you need a ride, pardner?"

I knew Kirk's voice even before I turned to look. He was wearing his Maxl's Deli apron, so I knew he'd just left work himself.

"Hi, Kirk," I said. "I was going to call my father for a ride, but if you're offering—"

"I am." He picked up the puppet stage as though it were lightweight, and carried it to the old blue car.

Here we go again, I thought. But I was too

weary to dwell on my feelings about being with Kirk.

"I'm just on my supper break from the deli," Kirk said after we'd gotten everything, including ourselves, into the car. "People kept coming into the deli all day, talking about the terrific puppet show on Main Street, so I had to take a look for myself. I knew it'd be you, Abby."

"Mmm. I managed to get this job all by myself," I said, leaning back against the car seat. "I never had a chance to tell you about it."

"I told you you didn't really need your old manager anymore." Kirk was keeping his eyes carefully ahead as he drove.

"That's not true. You're the one with all the ideas and all the newspaper connections."

I stole a look at Kirk. I loved looking at his face because it had become so familiar to me, and so dear. But that afternoon he looked tired and a bit drawn.

"Hey, you haven't gotten any tan yet, Kirk," I said. "Have you forgotten? This is summer."

"I'm going to remedy that tomorrow. Going fishing. Can I take you and Stevie along?"

I wanted to say yes. I was *aching* to say yes. But I knew it wouldn't be a smart thing to do. "Thanks, but I'm afraid not. On Sunday we always spend time with Mom and Dad. It's the only day for real family togetherness."

"I understand," he said. "Another time, then—a weekday?"

"Maybe," I said. *Why doesn't he stop?* I thought. *Why can't I have a nice, uncomplicated summer and not have to spend time with a boy I can't have?*

He drove straight to my house and carried my equipment into the garage for me. Then he smiled in a teasing way, like a big brother. "I heard you went out with Scott again last night."

"What are you, a gossip columnist?"

"I get around. I hear things. Well, listen, what I really wanted to tell you, Abby, is this. Maxl wants to hire someone part-time to wait on customers for supper sandwiches and so on. He likes you, so I know you can get the job easily."

Just what I need, I thought in dismay. *Working with Kirk for the rest of the summer.*

"Why, thank you. I'll see how that would fit in with my mother's work schedule, and maybe I'll go talk to Maxl."

I had no intention of going for that job. But as it turned out, Dad's car broke down that week and needed extensive repair work. And then Mugsley had to go to the vet for surgery, nothing serious, but it was costly.

I saw the worried looks on my parents' faces and I knew things would be better if I had a more steady job.

So I became one of Maxl's waitresses before the next week was over.

The summer days began slipping away quickly. I'd never been so busy in my life. Every night Mom went to work at the hospital, and in the morning she'd plop into bed immediately, to catch some sleep. That left me to straighten up the house, take care of Stevie, and try to do outdoor things like caring for Mom's flowers.

I also had to keep careful track of my puppet show schedule. There were several birthday parties, which in turn led to several more. By now they'd become easy for me to do. I had my scripts memorized and had the whole process down to a routine.

On the Saturday of the English fair, though, I was a little nervous because I'd never done Punch and Judy before. My father helped me set up the stage on the side lawn of the library.

The librarians and the children helpers came dressed in costumes from many periods of English history—long gowns on the girls, Robin Hood clothes for the boys mostly. It made a very colorful fair, along with the brightly colored tents and trade shops where experts demonstrated blacksmithing and other crafts.

It was fun, really.

The librarians all said that my puppet show

was a hit, and I think they were right because I certainly had my share of the audiences throughout the day. I thought they'd all be horrified by Punch's antics, but instead there was a lot of laughter—even when the baby flew out the window.

"I heard you did a terrific job at the library fair," Kirk told me the next time we were at work together. I was busy learning the ropes as a delicatessen waitress, and he was doing his stint at sandwich making behind the counter.

"How did you hear that?"

"Colleen told me. She stopped by the library for a book and went to watch your Punch and Judy show. But"—and here Kirk wagged a finger at me—"she said you never peeked your face out from behind the curtain, Abigail."

I laughed. "I guess I didn't. I told you I'd rather be invisible, whenever possible."

Maxl overheard us and grumbled, "How can such a pretty girl be invisible? Is impossible. Not a good idea, Abby."

"She *is* too pretty to hide behind a curtain, isn't she, Maxl?" Kirk was looking at me in that intense way he sometimes had, but only for a moment. He went back to slicing tomatoes.

"You have a good sense of humor," Maxl told

me. "We are teasing you, and you are a good sport, Abby."

That's me, I thought. *A good sport. I've been trying to be a good sport ever since the day a certain blond boy leaped into my raft.*

And it wasn't getting any easier.

Chapter Twelve

Working with Kirk was exquisite torture. There's no other way to put it. He was perfect: cheerful, hardworking, fun to be with—and impossible to be with.

I worked three evenings a week at Maxl's Deli, and it should have been pleasant. I'd never had a real job before, and I enjoyed catering to customers, receiving tips, and learning how to balance trays of gigantic sandwiches and soft drinks.

But there were those times when I'd look up and see Kirk, his blond head bent over his work, and my heart would actually stop for a moment. Or we'd be rushing in the bustle of a large supper-time crowd, and we'd bump into each other, our arms brushing lightly. And I'd always turn crimson from just that innocent bit of physical contact.

"For two cents I'd quit that job," I confided to Jan one night when I was sleeping over at her house.

"It's rough, hmm?" Jan did seem to understand when she wasn't wrapped up in her thoughts of Joe.

"It seems so unfair. I have so much feeling for Kirk, and that Colleen—well, she always seems too busy to spend much time with him. He must be lonely, or else why would he drop over to my house so often?"

"He does sound lonely—or confused," Jan agreed. "Well, Abby, maybe all you have to do is hang in there. Maybe one of these days they'll break up. And then you'll be right on the scene."

"Fat chance," I muttered. "Those two are welded together forever. Class ring, ID bracelets, you name it."

"Those are just *things*, Abby. Inanimate objects. They don't mean anything permanent. Even marriages break up sometimes."

I sighed. "Not those two. I'm afraid I'm doomed, Jan. I'm doomed to being his Chinese life partner for all eternity."

I had a puppet show to perform at the Shady Oaks Creative Arts Camp, which was in the next town from us, Marshdale. It was a morning performance, so I'd have to take Stevie with me.

And when Kirk heard about it, he offered to drive us there. I still hadn't gotten my driver's license.

On the way over, Kirk and Stevie talked happily about when they'd go fishing together. "I have a secret cove in the lake," Kirk told him. "A place that hardly anybody else knows about. It's quiet, and we can float around in my little rowboat and just relax."

"You don't know Stevie," I said cynically. "He's only three, Kirk. He doesn't sit still ever. Not anywhere. I think this plan of yours is destined for failure."

"We'll see," Kirk said, smiling in his usual cheerful way.

There was total bedlam at the Shady Oaks camp when we arrived. They had two hundred campers, all swarming around to see the puppeteer and her equipment. I got the impression they were a wealthy, spoiled bunch, but I had to be nice to them, anyway. They were my bread and butter for the day.

Kirk helped me set up the puppet stage at the appointed place, outside the main building, and he stayed to work the music for me.

The show didn't go so well as the others I'd done recently. The audience just wasn't as receptive. They were big-city kids evidently. They'd seen it all, and nothing I did was new or exciting for them. There was none of the laughing or cheering that I'd had from the local birthday parties.

"Well, you can't win them all, Abby," Kirk told me after we'd finished. The campers were already dispersing, leaving without a kind word to the puppeteer. It was depressing: I'd never had a failure before.

"Guess I'll have to work up more sophisticated plays for kids like these," I said philosophically. "Hey, Kirk, did you see where Stevie was sitting?"

"Yeah, he was right in front. I told him not to leave that spot." Kirk did a double take. "He's not there," he said grimly, and carefully put down the equipment he was holding.

We both made an effort not to panic. We searched calmly and quickly, to make sure that Stevie was not nearby. We called his name loudly, and we looked through the bushes and ran into the main house.

Stevie was nowhere in the area.

"Can you get any campers to help us?" I begged the camp director who'd hired me. "My little brother—he's only three, and he seems to have wandered off."

The director called back a number of the campers. He gave them instructions—along with my description of Stevie in his little faded jeans and blue sneakers—to search the camp in a hurry. Some of them groaned and complained, but most of them were willing to help.

I was terrified. It was the worst moment of my entire life, including being adrift on a raft in white water. I pictured all sorts of horrible things that could've happened to Stevie—and then I blotted them out because they were too awful to contemplate. I concentrated on the search.

Kirk took over. He organized the campers, barking out commands and getting their cooperation. He patted me quickly on the shoulder. "We'll find him, Abby," he reassured me.

And then we split up to cover more ground. I went stumbling up a rocky path that seemed to lead to the campers' cabins. There were tears streaming down my cheeks as I called out Stevie's name over and over again.

The woods seemed to close in around me. Those tall, dark trees seemed so ominous when I thought of a small boy alone and lost among them.

It was almost ten minutes later, though it seemed like hours, when Kirk and I met again at a fork in the path.

"Let's think, Abby. Where would he be likely to go?"

"You're right. Let's use logic. Stevie is not the type to wander off by himself."

"So maybe he followed some kid." Kirk's face looked as somber as I'd ever seen it. "I remember he was sitting next to a boy in a brown shirt and brown shorts."

We grabbed one of the campers who came along the path just then and asked about the boy in brown.

"That sounds like one of the Brown Elves—they're the youngest kids in the camp. They wear brown uniforms sometimes."

"Where is the Brown Elf campground?" Kirk asked impatiently.

The boy pointed, and we began to run along the path, back the way we'd come. The Brown Elves lived in cabins, rather than tents, near the lake.

We found Stevie sitting alone on a rock near a Brown Elves cabin. I swooped down on him, smothering him with kisses, while Kirk was demanding to know why he'd run away.

"I didn't run away," he insisted. "The boy was taking me to see his house. But he ran away. I waited here for you, Kerp."

Relief and gratitude flooded over me in an overwhelming tide. Stevie was safe, and that was all that mattered.

We marched him back to the puppet area. "I can't wait to get out of this place," Kirk said through clenched teeth. "If we never see Shady Oaks camp again, it'll be too soon."

I stared up at him. He sounded so much like a worried father. And then it hit me: for a little while we had been almost like a family. We'd been united by a fear even more immediate than the experience in the river raft. And Kirk had been absolutely invaluable in finding Stevie.

And I love Kirk so much, I thought suddenly, shocked at the intensity of my feelings. I loved him, I realized, more than I would ever love any other boy in my whole life.

And it was hopeless. A lost cause.

"You look so intense, Abby," Kirk said suddenly, looking at me worriedly. "Are you all right? I know what an ordeal it's been."

I had to say something. "I'll be OK. I was just thinking about"—I hesitated—"how much I seem to depend on you, Kirk. It seems as though whenever I need help, there you are." I could feel my face burning. "I never know how to thank you."

And then he looked at me as though I'd said something that really touched him.

"You don't have to thank me, Abby," he murmured and turned his face away, so that I couldn't see it. He appeared to be staring far off into the pine forest.

"I want to go home," Stevie wailed.

"We do, too," I told him. "And we're going, Stevie. Right now."

That evening, working at Maxl's, Kirk was grumpy. It was as though he didn't want to know me.

OK, have it your way, I thought defiantly. I pretended that I didn't know him either. I just kept busy with my duties, smiling at everyone and being a perfectly charming waitress.

Maxl noticed that something was odd. "What is this?" he asked, smacking Kirk on the back. "Two good friends do not speak to each other all night long?" When neither of us answered him, he told us that we were to stop working for a half-hour supper break.

"Take a sandwich, each of you, and go and talk," Maxl insisted.

Reluctantly we packed our supper, grabbed two sodas from the cooler, and left the mall.

"So? You want to walk down by the river?" Kirk asked. We were only two blocks from the main bridge into Brookdale.

"Sure." I shrugged to show that I didn't care.

We walked in silence, and when we reached the shore of the slow-moving river, we plunked down under one of the lush willow trees that grew every thirty feet or so.

"You don't have to talk to me," I said haughtily, unwrapping my sandwich. "I can see that you're a grouch tonight, Kirk."

He didn't answer.

"In fact, you don't have to eat with me," I went on. "I can move down the river a few more trees and leave you to your solitude."

Kirk snorted. "Don't be silly, Abby. My mood doesn't have anything to do with you."

"It doesn't?" I'd decided his mood was connected with our morning at the camp, that I had embarrassed him with my confession.

"No, I'm just making some decisions. And I spoke to my parents again, which is not always a pleasant thing to do."

I stared at him. "What's going on? Is it about college?"

"Yes." His face looked grim. "I've been telling them I didn't want to go to college at all. But now I've realized that I do need college. I just don't want to be a lawyer."

"And what do they say to that?"

"They're having fits, of course. But what I told them is this. I really enjoyed writing the publicity for your puppet shows. I loved contacting the newspapers and setting up the flyers for the printer, everything about the publicity."

I frowned, not understanding where he was leading.

"Don't you see? I decided I want to go into public relations, Abby, or some kind of advertising, where I can use my art skills, my photography, and the writing that I enjoy so much."

My face must have lit up in a big, bright way. "But that's wonderful, Kirk," I said. "I can't think of anything better for you."

His eyes clouded over. "My parents don't see it that way. They may come around, eventually. Right now they're too upset. They had counted on a dynasty of lawyers, you know? My two older brothers and then me. But when the shock wears off, it's possible that all will be forgiven."

I took a bite of my supper. So this was what was on Kirk's mind—not anything about me.

"I hope it works out for you, Kirk," I said. *I thought you might have sensed my feelings for you,* my mind cried out even as I called myself a total fool.

It was just as well that he hadn't.

Chapter Thirteen

August had arrived, with its long, hot days and beautiful, star-studded nights.

"We've all been working like slaves this summer," Suzi declared, admiring herself in the mirror in her hallway. "So we deserve a treat like this. Really we do."

She was referring to her Summer Dream Ball, which was to begin in exactly half an hour. Jan and I had been at Suzi's house all day, helping her set up for the party, and now we'd all showered and changed into our dresses.

Mine was borrowed from my cousin Cathleen, and it was easily the most beautiful dress I'd ever worn. It was cocktail length, with a smooth, satiny, white bodice, and spaghetti straps. The skirt billowed out in layers of rich white lace. My mother had added a wide red satin ribbon—"to accentuate your slim waist."

Jan had intertwined baby's breath with her long, dark, straight hair in an elaborate french braid. She really looked sensational—tall and slim now, in a long gown of blue taffeta. She glowed with health and happiness.

Suzi looked great, as she always did, in a soft pink, very expensive gown that was cut low at the neckline. Her eye shadow and nail polish exactly matched the shade of her gown. This party was going to be a treat.

Our dates arrived together: Al for Suzi, Joe for Jan, and Scott for me. They all wore suits, and they all looked properly impressed when they saw us in our formal dresses.

"Is this my racquetball partner?" Joe bellowed when he saw Jan looking so slim and feminine. "Is this really my buddy who always wears sweat pants and sneakers?" Then he stopped clowning and planted a kiss on her nicely tanned nose. And she gave him a playful hug.

Al, the strong, silent type, said nothing, but Scott whispered, "You look beautiful, Abby." He really was sweet.

I led Scott out to the Brownings' patio, where a canopy had been set up in case of rain. But there was no rain on the horizon that night. We'd strung Japanese lanterns and arranged a long elegant buffet table. Suzi's parents had even hired a DJ to play records.

Couple after couple began arriving. Suzi had invited a really large crowd, and the turnout was amazing. Who would have thought that so many kids would want to dress up in formal clothes in the middle of summer?

"You girls did a great job, Abby," Scott said, admiring the decorations and the elegance of the Brownings' large patio. "Would you like to dance?"

When the music started, I stepped into Scott's arms and tried to forget all the little things that had been making me uneasy this summer. Kirk, most of all. I smiled brightly for Scott and answered his questions about my latest puppet shows—several birthday parties, a Girl Scout show, and a demonstration at the library on how to create papier-mâché puppet heads.

The party became noisier and more crowded. I could see Jan whirling around with Joe, smiling up at him with a look of real love. Joe still did a lot of teasing, but he was different lately, too; with his trimmed-down body, he was acquiring new self-confidence.

About an hour into the party, the moment I'd been dreading arrived. Kirk and Colleen showed up. I had actually begged Suzi not to invite them, but she was adamant; they couldn't be left off the guest list.

Both of them greeted us as they began dancing across the patio. Colleen was wearing a flowered print dress, with bare shoulders, and she looked stunning as only a tall redhead can among the rest of us Munchkins.

I won't watch them at all, I decided, turning my attention to Scott. If I keep my eyes away from them, then I can pretend they aren't here. And it can't hurt at all.

But late in the evening Kirk came looking for me.

"A dance, Abby?" He looked first at me and then at Scott for permission. "We have business to discuss—big important corporate stuff, about Maxl's new shipment of sauerkraut."

I was a total wreck in just those short seconds before Kirk's arms went around me. I went cold all over, and my heart was pounding like a jackhammer. I wondered if he could hear it thumping.

"Relax, Abby," Kirk whispered. "You don't mind dancing with me, do you?"

"Well, that depends," I quipped, throwing my head back. "Are you going to step on my feet?"

He smiled. "Nah, your feet look too pretty in those white shoes. In fact, all of you looks great.

The white dress makes you look like, well, like a bride. Am I being corny?"

"As corny as Kansas in August," I answered, swallowing hard and hiding my emotions pretty well, I thought. Kirk danced slowly, holding me with a firm touch, and it felt as though his hand were burning a hole in my back.

He was so familiar to me, yet this was the first time he'd held me for dancing. His body felt so firm and warm, and up close like that he smelled clean and masculine. I was horrified at the way I was reacting. I wanted more than anything just to press my face against his jacket, just for a short moment.

I'm not sure what happened then. But somehow we drifted into the shadows of the far edge of the patio, near a flowering shrub where no Japanese lanterns lit the area.

And we were as close as any two people can be, on a dance floor. I found myself resting my head against Kirk's strong chest. You couldn't have put a matchstick between us.

There was no talking now. There was only the soft, pulsing music and the beautiful summer night, with stars overhead and the perfume of the August flowers.

We feel so right together, I thought with a real, physical ache in my heart. And it was true. Kirk and I shared so much those days: our jobs together at the deli and our trips to puppet shows together in his blue car; his dropping over at my house, playing with Stevie and talking with my parents. We had even gone fishing once, to Kirk's secret cove. Stevie had ruined it, as I'd predicted, by crashing around in the boat, until finally we gave up. But it had been a pleasant morning just the same.

How could two people have so much in common and not be in love? That was the question that tormented me. And in the end I always had to face the cold, hard facts: Kirk was not attracted to me. He was in love with Colleen.

But for now, for this one superb, enchanted moment, we were dancing closely and not saying a word.

"Hey, you two," called out a new, cheerfully discreet Joe Dalton. He had guided Jan across the dance floor to our corner. "I hate to say this, but you're causing quite a sensation."

"What?" Kirk's head snapped up. So did mine. Half the kids at the party stood watching us as we swayed back and forth.

And there was Colleen, a cool, controlled expression on her face. She was standing entirely alone by the buffet table, staring at us. There was no way of telling what was on her mind.

"Uh, I guess this number is over, Abby." Kirk

spoke matter-of-factly, and I couldn't tell what he was thinking, either.

I pulled away. I only knew that the number definitely was over—for us.

The next morning, when I went down to breakfast, my mother told me that Colleen had telephoned.

"She said to give you a message," Mom said. "She's coming over to see you in half an hour. Wants to know if you'd like to go for a ride."

I must have stared, bug eyed. My heart was doing flipflops. "Colleen? Is coming here?"

"That's what she said. Why? Don't you like her?"

"I like her. But—why in the world does she want to see me? Unless—unless she's furious about last night." And then I had to explain to my mother what had happened at the party.

"So what does a student psychologist make of that?" I asked when I'd finished.

Mom shook her head. "I don't know, hon. I don't think the college had a course for a problem this complicated."

"Oh, great!" I groaned. "You're no help. Here's this big, angry girlfriend of Kirk's coming over, maybe to kill me, and you have no solutions."

"I'm sure no one is going to kill you, Abby. You've been the innocent party in this whole situation. You've been nothing but a friend to Kirk, and I'm sure Colleen is aware of that."

Nothing but a friend. Then why had we danced like that? I wondered. How in the world had that happened, anyway?

I was scared out of my mind when Colleen arrived, and it was just lucky that Mom was there to make small talk for a few minutes. I jammed my hands into my jeans pockets and stood there, silent, until we went off in Colleen's car.

Colleen got right to the point. "I know you must think it's peculiar, my coming over like this, Abby. Especially without giving you a chance to say no."

"Well, sure, I—I was curious."

She drove to the end of my street and stopped the car. "This isn't really a joy ride," she said. "I wanted to talk to you."

"What—what about?"

"About Kirk, of course." Her face was unreadable.

"Kirk and I are just friends, Colleen," I blurted out stupidly, instead of waiting to see what she'd say.

Colleen blinked in surprise. "Why, of course you are, Abby. I wasn't going to suggest otherwise. But the thing is, you've been such a good friend to him that I wonder if I can ask a favor of you?"

"A favor?"

"Yes. I'm going away on vacation Monday, with my whole family. We go to Newport, Rhode Island, every summer for two weeks at the beach. And Kirk is going to be so alone while I'm gone. I wondered if you'd keep him company, as much as possible?"

I almost choked. "You're kidding," I said bluntly. "You've got to be kidding. No girl ever asks another girl to keep her boyfriend company."

"Oh, Abby." Colleen laughed as if I'd said something hilarious. "I know Kirk will be safe with you. And I'd feel much better about leaving him if I knew he had someone to go to a movie with once in a while."

"I don't know, Colleen. Why doesn't he do things with other boys? Like Joe, or some of the other guys in his class?"

"Oh, he will, I imagine. But he really likes being with you. He says you're so much fun. And I just want to say that it's all right with me. I'd like to see you two spend some time together."

It was crazy. It was certainly unexpected. I kept staring at Colleen to see what she could be thinking.

"Well, that's settled, then?" Colleen gave me a great big smile. "You just go out with Kirk wher-

ever you want—movies, beach, or dancing—
whatever. And I'll feel really good the whole time
I'm away in Rhode Island."

No, I wanted to say. *No, this is not a good idea.*

But I remained silent. It was impossible to
argue. I didn't want her guessing why I was so
reluctant.

Chapter Fourteen

So my dilemma became more complex. I was in love with Kirk, and his girlfriend had given us her blessing to be together.

I just won't do it, I thought firmly. He can be as lonely as he wants, but nothing is going to make me go out with him.

My resolve didn't last, of course. The first time Kirk called, I melted.

"Can I talk you into a movie, Abby?" He sounded different this time over the telephone. He wasn't calling to talk about puppets or publicity, or Maxl's deli. He was asking me for an actual date.

We went to see a movie that was dripping with romance. It was almost embarrassing because there was such a deep love between the hero and heroine. By the time the screen said The End, I was sniffling into a tissue.

"Didn't know you were such a romantic, Abby," Kirk said, teasing me.

"I didn't know it, either," I answered, blowing my nose, which I was sure was bright red. "Usually Jan is the one who cries in the movies."

"And you hardly touched your popcorn," Kirk commented as we walked up the aisle with the rest of the crowd.

Being with you makes me lose my appetite, I was thinking, but I said nothing. I had been sitting there wondering what it would be like to have Kirk hold my hand. I'd been fantasizing about him—his putting his arm around the back of my chair, then across my shoulders . . .

"I ought to get home now," I ventured. "I have to be up early in the morning, you know. To take care of Stevie while Mom gets her sleep."

"Oh, it's still early. I bet you never go home this early when you're out with that Scott guy."

"Well, actually, when we double-date with Jan and Joe, they make us walk after a movie. For exercise, you know."

"So that's what we'll do now. How about it? A quick walk down to the river, where we ate our supper that night? It should be really pretty tonight."

"I don't think so." But I knew I was weakening.

"Come on, just a half-hour walk." He grabbed my hand and pulled me along Main Street toward the riverbank.

It was a dark night, with no moon and no visible stars. The street lamps cast an eerie glow on us. I felt as if we were completely alone in the universe. It was a peculiar experience.

I started to jabber. I talked about Kirk's decision to go into public relations. I told him about the latest calls I'd gotten for puppet shows. I mentioned that my mother really liked her job, surprisingly, but that she had firm plans for going back, part-time, to her psychology classes in the fall.

"You sure can talk a lot, Abby," Kirk said, laughing. "You're awfully jumpy tonight."

"Not at all. I told Colleen that I'd keep you company, and I'm trying to keep you entertained. If you'd rather have me shut up, I can do that, too."

We were standing on the riverbank now, looking out over the satiny blackness of the water. Overhead, the weeping willows bent their trailing branches toward us, casting long shadows from the light of the street lamps.

Kirk was still holding my hand. I thought I ought to pull it away, out of loyalty to Colleen, but there was a perverse little devil in me that kept saying, *I like this.*

"So Colleen made you promise to date me, hmm?" Kirk seemed to find that amusing. "What do you make of that, Abby?"

"Frankly, I think she's crazy."

He laughed. "Why?"

I looked sideways at him. "Because. If I had a boyfriend like you, I'd never want him to spend time with some other girl. Even if she was short and young and unsophisticated."

Kirk was silent for a moment. "Is that how you see yourself—as so inferior? I suppose you think Colleen's got it all, just because she's taller and—what? Sophisticated?"

"You're darned right, she's got it all."

"Abby." Kirk was moving closer to me, and I was suddenly unable to ignore him any longer. Not that I wanted to.

"Abby," he said again more quietly, and his hand reached under my chin to raise my face ever so slightly. In the light from the street lamp I could see his eyes—sober and thoughtful, very much in control of what he was about to do.

He kissed me. His lips were cool and feathery light, barely brushing my lips. And then he hesitated, as if to gauge my reaction, I suppose.

I was so stunned and so overwhelmed that I put out my free hand to touch the collar of his shirt. And that was all he needed.

Kirk's lips came down on mine once again,

still gentle, but this time confident, assured, as if he was not at all surprised. And although I knew that it was wrong, I gave myself up to that one kiss.

Because it would be the only one we'd ever, ever have. I knew that.

I remembered how I had wondered, after my birthday party, when my first kiss would occur. Here it was, and it was tinged with sadness.

Still, it was my very first kiss, and it lasted for a long time. I loved the way Kirk's mouth felt; it was as though I'd always known exactly how it would be. I wished that kiss could go on forever.

But there was a definite shadow between us—the shadow of Colleen—and so, finally, I pulled away. And I summoned up great anger.

"You have some nerve!" I howled. "Is that the way you operate? Your girlfriend is away just three days, and already you're out trying to make other conquests?"

"Oh, Abby, cut it out. You know I'm not—"

"Don't even speak to me, Kirk Phillips. This is the final straw! You've been talking about Chinese life partners for a long time now, and I believed you. No strings attached—hah! It was all a bunch of garbage, wasn't it? All you want to do is take my heart and twist it and watch it break into little pieces."

"Are you crazy? I never, never intended for this to happen." He sounded genuinely confused.

"Don't give me that. I'm telling you right now, Kirk, that our friendship is through. Through! There is no way I will ever see you again or go out with you—day or night."

"Abby, we've been such good friends. What about the puppet shows? What about all the things we've done?"

"Over." I spoke with firm finality. "It's all history, pal. I don't need you in my life—not as a Chinese life partner and not as a friend. Not as anything, Kirk."

Of course, I didn't mean a word of it. I loved him. I loved him so much that I was hurting all over. But I had reached the end of my rope. I had to make a clean break with this boy, for my own survival.

"Come off it, Abby. You're overreacting. I guess maybe I shouldn't have kissed you, but you seemed to like it, you know."

"Take me home, Kirk." I spoke coldly and started to walk away from him. "If you don't, I'll go to the nearest telephone and call my father. He'll come for me."

Kirk began to realize that I was serious. He followed me, and we marched in silence back toward the Main Street parking lot. I climbed into his car and held my head up high.

"Abby, what was so terrible about that kiss? We've been friends. Why shouldn't we have human emotions?"

"Human emotions!" I exploded. "That really does it. You think you can experiment with my emotions? Well, no, thanks. I have feelings, you know. And right now my feeling is that I'm never going to put up with you again."

Kirk narrowed his eyes. "Put up with me?"

"That's right. Now will you start this car? I want to go home, I said. I've put up with all your butting into my life and trying to run it. But now it's over. Finished."

I guess I got to him with that. A dark shadow slid across his face. He stopped trying to argue. He raced the motor, then drove slowly, deliberately at a snail's pace, toward my house.

"I never knew I was such a nuisance to you, Abby," he said after a long silence. He was trying to keep his voice even, and not succeeding.

"Well, now you know it. I was happy before you came along, Kirk. Things were just fine."

He had pulled into my driveway.

"Good night then, Abby. And—I'm sorry. Believe me, I'll never bother you again. Never."

I stepped out of his car, and he drove away. He was gone. Just like that.

I was shattered.

You did what you had to do, I told myself.

But I just couldn't go into the house yet. I needed a few minutes alone in the quiet, dark night to remember that kiss in every detail and then to agonize over the finality of our argument.

"You were truly a rat to kiss me like that, Kirk," I whispered with bitter tears rolling down my cheeks. "But I love you. And, oh, how I will miss you."

Chapter Fifteen

"He was a rat, Abby, to kiss you like that." Suzi spoke with great wisdom and certainty as she plucked away at her eyebrows in front of Jan's bedroom mirror. "You did the right thing, staging that fight."

Jan was less certain. "Maybe he has some kind of feelings for Abby, though," she said romantically. "Maybe he just couldn't help himself. Maybe it had come to a point where he wanted to compare Abby with Colleen—"

"Oh, Jan, grow up!" Suzi loved that expression. "The boy thinks he can have his cake and eat it, too. Well, that's just not good enough for our Abby."

Nobody, it seemed, cared what I thought. So I just sat there dismally, not saying a word. I wasn't sure what I thought. All I knew was that I was thoroughly, utterly miserable.

Kirk and I weren't even working together at the deli. The first evening I went back after our fight, Maxl told me that Kirk had decided to take a job offer at the Village Camera Shop instead. Maxl was sorry to lose such a good worker, but he knew that Kirk was eager to learn more about photography.

So Kirk was gone from there, too, and without even giving Maxl two weeks' notice. I felt responsible. I knew that if I hadn't lashed out at him like that, he wouldn't have left the deli.

"Don't worry, Abby. We can still have fun together," Jan said, giving me a reassuring smile. "Scott likes you a lot, and we can double-date anytime you want."

"I don't think so, Jan," I mumbled. "I don't seem to have much interest in Scott. It wouldn't be fair to lead him on. I know how it feels to love someone who will never love you in return."

"Oh, this is too tragic to talk about," Suzi declared. She didn't like it when any of us discussed deep problems. "Let's talk about something else instead. How about the football team?"

"How about if you two talk about football?" I suggested evenly. "I think I'll just go on home. I have to make a batch of new puppets, anyway. I have a show to do at the White Elephant Flea Market on Saturday."

"Oh, how nice, Abby," Suzi gushed. "You see? You have plenty to keep you busy. You won't be feeling sad for long at all."

I smiled thinly at Suzi. I said goodbye to both of them, knowing that they'd discuss Kirk and me for a while after I'd gone, at least until Suzi became bored with the discussion.

The rest of that summer was highlighted only by my puppet shows. Every Saturday I did shows at the flea market, and people would drop money into a basket if they liked the show. There was quite a bit of change at the end of every day.

When the new Brookdale Shopping Mall opened, I was there to promote opening day for that. Again there was newspaper publicity, but not promoted by Kirk. I found myself missing his ever-present camera and his offers of rides home.

I missed *him*. The friend who had turned into so much more for me. And I hated myself for that romantic weakness. If only I hadn't fallen in love with Kirk, we would still be pals, the way he intended it to be.

Why had I been so stupid?

I did several special shows in the pediatrics section of Brookdale Hospital. My mother arranged those. I didn't get any pay, but it was rewarding to help make the hospitalized kids laugh, all those children in pajamas and robes, some with crutches and some with intravenous tubes attached to their arms.

An odd thing happened at the third show I did in pediatrics. I was finishing a Punch and Judy skit when I looked out from behind the curtain—I don't really know why—and I could have sworn I saw Kirk.

I blinked, not believing. There was this tall, blond boy standing outside the glass partition of the ward, just looking in with a solemn expression on his face. It *had* to be Kirk. And yet, when I looked again just seconds later, he was gone.

I realized it couldn't have been Kirk; he didn't even know about the hospital shows. I was fooling myself. Would I ever stop thinking of him?

Summer came to a close. Mom was excited because she was enrolling at college for two courses. Stevie would go to the day-care center five mornings a week, so Mom could work and get her sleep in the mornings. He was ecstatic about being a "real school kid," complete with a tiny lunchbox for his morning snack.

Our family finances were better now because Dad was working some overtime again, and Mom decided to keep her hospital job. My parents insisted that I resign from the deli for the school year, because with schoolwork and the puppets I had plenty to keep me busy.

Maxl told me to come back next summer, if I needed a job then. "I will miss you—and Kirk," he said, shaking his head sadly. "You are both nice young people. And I think that there should not be trouble between you two, Abby."

"I can't help it, Maxl," I said, wondering how he always seemed to know so much about Kirk and me.

"That Colleen—she is not the right girl for Kirk," Maxl declared, frowning. When he was serious, he resembled one of the chubby characters on his beer steins. "Now you—with you, Abby, I see a much happier Kirk. This is what I see."

I smiled at him. "You can't be a matchmaker, Maxl. Better stick to making liverwurst sandwiches."

"We will see," Maxl said stubbornly. "We will see."

I started back to school that first day determined to put on a cheerful face even though my heart felt very heavy. I walked, as always, with Jan and Suzi. Both of them were trying to keep me from brooding about Kirk, but it was no use.

I knew that I'd be seeing the Golden Couple everywhere I went in the halls of Brookdale High.

It was Joe Dalton who rushed over to us, just before the opening day assembly, to tell us the news.

"You're not going to believe this," he said, his voice low. "But guess who broke up. Kirk and Colleen."

The whole school seemed to be buzzing about it. Nobody had any idea why, but apparently it was the truth. Colleen had given back Kirk's class ring, and Kirk was no longer wearing the ID bracelet on his wrist.

I was so stunned that I didn't know what to think.

"What happened with them, Joe?" Jan kept asking. She was dying to hear all the details.

"Kirk won't talk about it. Neither will Colleen. I can't tell you a thing." Joe shrugged. "Mystery of the year, I guess."

Nothing changed, though, as far as Kirk's talking to me. When I did see him, he would nod politely or maybe just throw me a "hi" as though I were somebody he had once known a long time ago.

Colleen was more friendly. She'd wave profusely or yell out, "Hi, there, Abby!" whenever we passed in the hall. But we had no classes together and never had an opportunity to talk.

I was a junior now, and it felt different being an upperclassman. And one odd thing had happened: because of my puppet career, I was no longer invisible at Brookdale High. Kids approached me all the time to say that they'd read about me in the newspaper or that they'd seen one of my shows at one place or another. My name and face were known, and that was a peculiar feeling.

It wasn't exactly popularity, but it was a chance to make new friends, and that's what I tried to do. I used each conversation as an opportunity to be cheerful and open. Mom had suggested that. "You mature that way, Abby. By caring about each and every person who crosses your path. And if you show a little warmth, without expecting anything in return, why, you'll be surprised at the rewards you'll get—rewards of the heart."

She was right. I was changing in a subtle way. I wasn't afraid of my own shadow anymore. I had a new sense of self-confidence. People liked me.

But I didn't like myself much.

I had this terrible nagging guilt about Kirk. It was more than just the fact that I missed him. A little voice inside me kept saying, "You *hurt* him, Abby, and he didn't deserve that. Kirk is a kind, decent human being, and you dealt him a karate chop that was downright vicious."

I kept seeing his shadowed face on that night when I'd told him to stop butting into my life. Why had I phrased it like that? I'd said that I was never going to put up with him again, and that he'd been trying to run things.

My stomach knotted every time I thought of what I had said that awful evening. Then I'd remember the boy behind the glass partition at the hospital ward not wanting me to see him. It had been Kirk, I was sure, and he had been hiding from me.

It was that image that made me realize just how very deeply I must have hurt him.

Finally after school had been in session for about a week, I knew that I had to do something about it.

Chapter Sixteen

On a quiet September Sunday morning, I left my house, wearing my newest jeans, my prettiest pale blue sweater, and a tiny gold marionette charm on a chain.

Indian summer had taken hold, with warm, balmy breezes and the beginnings of golden color in the tree leaves. I had a driver's license now, so I drove Mom's car to a secluded parking spot near the lake.

And there was the beat-up old blue car, parked where it usually was when Kirk went to fish in his secret cove. I only hoped that he was alone. If he had a new girlfriend with him, or if he was reunited with Colleen, then I'd slip quietly away. What I had to say was for Kirk alone.

I kept peering through the shoreline hemlocks, trying to catch a glimpse of Kirk's little boat. No luck.

He must have gone into the deep part of the lake, I thought. I wouldn't find him for hours, if at all.

But I kept searching, tiptoeing along from one shrub to the next, hoping. I came to the end of the cove, and still no Kirk. At least not in my view.

I sighed. *Should I give up, or should I wait?* Sooner or later he'd come rowing back, wouldn't he? Even if I had to wait all morning.

But suddenly there he was. Rowing slowly back into the cove. My pulse quickened. My courage was failing fast. I could leave quickly, and he'd never know I'd been there.

No. I had done something wrong, and I had to make amends. I liked to think that I had done a lot of growing up over the summer. Well, here was my chance to prove it.

Kirk and his boat came closer to where I was hiding behind a wild honeysuckle bush. I could see his face, so familiar and so dear to me. But it was not a happy face.

I remembered how I'd always thought of Kirk as eternally happy. There was nothing happy about him now. He simply looked drained and tired.

I wondered if Colleen had done that to him.

Why had they broken up, anyway? Perhaps I'd never know. But at any rate, that was not why I was there.

"I'd like to leap into your boat," I called out as loudly as I could manage. I emerged from behind the bush. "The same way you jumped into my raft last spring. But I'd probably manage to capsize us both."

Kirk turned to stare, and the look on his face was one of astonishment. "Abby," was all he said. I think he was too surprised even to sound wary.

"I'm going to talk fast," I said, walking closer to the edge of the lake. "So I won't lose my nerve. Kirk, I'm here because I owe you an apology. And an explanation."

Now his face did look wary. "Explanation of what?"

I took a deep breath; I needed it. "I want to explain why I picked that fight with you that night we went to the movies."

Kirk rowed slowly toward shore. "I believe you did explain at the time. You were furious because I kissed you. And you were tired of me pestering you."

"Will you please shut up and let me talk?" I stunned both of us with my assertiveness. "Kirk, it wasn't the fact that you kissed me, and it certainly wasn't true that you pestered

159

me—that was the furthest thing from the truth. It was—"

Another deep breath. "There's no easy way to say this, so I just have to blurt it out, and you can laugh if you want to. I—I started to care about you—too much. I guess I'm just a stupid adolescent girl who just couldn't control her feelings." I held up my hands to silence him. "I know how hopeless it was, but it happened, and I didn't know how to handle things."

He was silent, but I had to keep on talking. "Then when you kissed me, it just blew my mind, Kirk. There you were, playing some kind of a game while Colleen was away. and I—I was about ready to be committed to the funny farm!"

Kirk sat perfectly still in the boat; not a muscle moved in his face. His brown eyes were giving me full attention. *Well*, I thought, *at least he's not laughing at me.*

"Kirk, I just want to say that I'm so sorry. Picking that fight was the only way I could think of to—to end the situation that was causing me so much pain. I never stopped to consider that it was a rotten way to treat a friend. And you surely were a friend, a terrific pal, all summer long."

He put down the oars, and a slight smile twisted at the corners of his mouth. "Now wait," he finally said. "Let me get this straight. You came here to apologize about the fight, Abby?"

I nodded miserably. "Of course. I couldn't leave things the way they were, with those awful things I said still between us. And even if you don't want to forgive me, that's all right, too. I just had to try to make you understand, for my own peace of mind."

"I think I do understand, now." He spoke quietly and firmly. And then he stepped out of the boat, pulling it to shore and tying it to a tree.

Tears filled my eyes. "I don't know if we can ever be friends again, Kirk, but at least I'm glad you can see where I was coming from."

It was time for me to leave. I'd said what I had come to say. I was intruding on Kirk's private fishing time.

But Kirk put a hand on my arm so that I couldn't turn away. "This explains a lot of things about that night," he said in a low voice. "I was really bummed out for a while there, you know? And then I started to wish we could communicate again. You probably saw me there at the hospital."

I nodded wordlessly.

"Even today," Kirk went on. "I was thinking about you as I was rowing the boat, just before you appeared."

"You were?" I felt a surge of gladness. It seemed as though my apology was going to be accepted, after all. I said, "We really are Chinese life partners, Kirk."

"No." He reached out and touched my face with great gentleness. "No, I don't think that's it, Abby. Not anymore."

"No?" I prayed that I wouldn't start crying.

Kirk shrugged and took his hand away from my cheek. "It's hard to explain," he began as though he had a long tale to tell. "Colleen and I had been going together for so long that we were, well, just getting bored with each other, I think."

He kicked at a small rock on the path, but not angrily. "Neither of us wanted to admit it, but that's the way it was. And then when I met you, Abby, I began to realize that there was a better way to live. With real friendship, and laughter, and common interests."

He gave me a long, steady gaze that made me uncomfortable. "Above all, there was the way you seemed to appreciate me, and need me, and accept me, whereas Colleen really wanted me to be someone I'm not. . . ." Kirk's voice trailed off.

"Well, I do appreciate you," I said simply. "You have a great many talents, and you used them so generously to help me last summer. Even though I think of myself as pretty independent, it was so nice to have someone to lean on when I needed to."

Kirk said quietly, "It was nice to have someone lean on *me*, for the first time in my life."

"Did you break off with Colleen?" I asked.

He laughed. "That's the funny part. No. She was just as tired of going with me as I was tired of going with her. She was trying, the whole time, to encourage my interest in you."

"You're kidding," I managed to say. My mouth fell open with surprise.

"No, really. Colleen threw us together every chance she got, if you'll recall, and especially when she went away on vacation. There was some guy up there in Rhode Island who interested her. Well, anyway, when she came back, she told me that she wanted to date other people. We both agreed on that. We needed to call it off."

I was shaking my head, unable to digest all this at once. Colleen—the perfect, poised, intimidating Colleen—was not really the perfect girl for Kirk, after all!

I was very aware of being close to Kirk and of his hands now on my shoulders. Birds were chattering in the treetops overhead, but all I could focus on was Kirk—the nearness of his bulky tan sweater, and the clean scent of his hair, and the way his lips looked, there in the dappled woodsy light.

"I'm sorry you've been so unhappy," I finally said.

"You look as though you've been somewhat miserable yourself, kiddo."

And then I started to talk too much. "Do you think so? I shouldn't be. I've been very busy with the puppets, and everything's going fine at home, and the only thing that was terribly wrong was that I owed you this apology, so—"

"You're babbling," Kirk said softly, sounding amused.

"Sure. I do that when I get rattled. I never seem to know when to keep quiet. I—"

"How about keeping quiet now?" Kirk suggested, and he gathered me even closer into his strong arms. I found myself leaning my head against that beloved chest so that I could hear his heart beat.

It didn't feel strange at all. We had danced together this way once, at Suzi's party. Being in Kirk's arms had felt so right then, and that's how it felt now. Very right. It was my fantasy come true. And yet I couldn't believe that it was really happening.

"Abby, that night after the movies, I couldn't help that kiss. I wasn't playing games, not at all. I had fallen in love with you, but I didn't know how to say so. I think it actually happened way back on our raft ride."

"But, I never dreamed—" I whispered.

Just wait until Maxl hears about this, I

164

thought crazily. *And Jan—won't she love knowing that she was right about Kirk, all along!* Even Mom had known. All three of them had seen something that we hadn't. Or wouldn't allow ourselves to see.

"I guess I didn't realize what was happening," Kirk said simply. "All along I thought I just wanted you for a friend. With no strings." He grinned at that last phrase, his wonderful grin that I'd so longed to see again.

My heart went soaring with a joy that was simply too new, and too fragile, to describe.

"In a puppeteer's life there are always strings, silly." I reached up and traced my fingers along his cheekbone. "I love you too, Kerp. With lots and lots of strings."

And we kissed the second time with no shadows between us.

We hope you enjoyed reading this book. All the titles currently available in the Sweet Dreams series are listed on the next two pages. They are all available at your local bookshop or newsagent, though should you find any difficulty in obtaining the books you would like, you can order direct from the publisher, at the address below. Also, if you would like to know more about the series, or would simply like to tell us what you think of the series, write to:

Kim Prior,
Sweet Dreams,
Transworld Publishers Limited,
61–63 Uxbridge Road,
London W5 5SA.

To order books, please list the title(s) you would like, and send together with your name and address, and a cheque or postal order made payable to TRANSWORLD PUBLISHERS LIMITED. Please allow cost of book(s) plus 20p for the first book and 10p for each additional book for postage and packing.

(The above applies to readers in the UK and Ireland only.)

If you live in Australia or New Zealand, and would like more information about the series, please write to:

Sally Porter,
Sweet Dreams
Corgi & Bantam Books,
26 Harley Crescent,
Condell Park,
N.S.W. 2200,
Australia.

Kiri Martin
Sweet Dreams
c/o Corgi & Bantam Books
   New Zealand,
Cnr. Moselle and Waipareira
   Avenues,
Henderson,
Auckland,
New Zealand.